Y0-DKF-852

THE HANGING SHADOW

"We were shooting the hanging scene. Everything went perfectly. The director yelled 'cut,' and the grips rushed in to help Nedra down off the beam. They didn't want her to hang too long from the neck brace. The window behind her was still lighted. We could see the hanging shadow of Nedra, and the shadows of the grips as they reached up to take her down. Carter noticed something was wrong before I did, maybe it was the way Nedra's body looked so limp in the arms of the grips.
Anyway, he started running towards her before it dawned on me that anything was amiss. Then everything was in a panic. I tried to reach Carter, but I couldn't get through the crowd. So I kept asking what was wrong. I heard someone say, "Nedra was dead. Her neck was broken."

MIST OF EVIL

Patricia Matthews

DISCARD

Severn House

This title first published in Great Britain 1990 by
SEVERN HOUSE PUBLISHERS LTD of
35 Manor Road, Wallington, Surrey SM6 0BW

This first hardcover edition published in the U.S.A. 1990 by
SEVERN HOUSE PUBLISHERS INC, NEW YORK

Originally published in the U.S.A. in paperback format only by
Manor Books, Inc under the pseudonym Patty Brisco

Copyright © 1976 by Patty Brisco

All rights reserved. The right of Patricia Matthews to be identified
as author of this work has been asserted by her in accordance with
the Copyright, Designs and Patents Act 1988.

British Library Cataloguing in Publication Data

Matthews, Patricia *1927–*
   Mist of evil.
   I. Title
   813.54 [F]

   ISBN 0-7278-4110-6

Distributed in the U.S.A. by
Mercedes Distribution Center, Inc
62 Imlay Street, Brooklyn, New York 11231

Printed and bound in Great Britain by
the University Press, Cambridge

Chapter One

"Welcome to Trollhaugen, Molly!"

Carter smiled down at me and I smiled back from the shelter of his arms.

The moon was full, flooding the house with a mellow light. I could see it was all I had hoped it would be; a living embodiment of all my secret fantasies. Constructed of heavy grey stone, turreted and towered, cloaked with ivy and the patina of time, it looked like something conceived by Disney out of Dali. I loved it.

Carter leaned down and pressed his lips against my forehead. "I won't ask if you like it. The look on your face, sweetheart, makes it perfectly clear to me that you married me not for myself, but for my house."

I laughed and hugged him close. "It's wonderful, darling. But then, it had to be. It's yours."

I started for the steps, but Carter stopped me with a hand on my arm. "Wait!" he said. He leaned down and scooped me up in his arms. "Let's do this right."

Clasping my arms around his neck, I simpered down at him and even kicked my toes girlishly. I knew a good movie scene when I saw one. Carter, with only a slight grunt, carried me up the broad steps and stopped before the carved wooden door.

The door was huge—at least eight feet high and half as wide—and lovingly carved with an intricate pattern of leaves and flowers which had been smoothed by time and polished by weather. When I reached toward it to tug the bell pull, my hand looked fragile and pale against the dark oak wood. I had no sooner drawn my hand back than the door began to swing open. I took a firmer grip on Carter's neck as I tried not to anticipate what the house would look like inside, yet it would be no exaggeration to say that I was filled with anticipation. This was the happiest day of my life.

The door slid open smoothly, and I wondered if my hair was mussed. I was eager to make a good impression on Mr. Alexander, the houseman Carter had told me about.

Then, as the door opened all the way, I felt the smile freeze into an expression of terror. I kicked downward and away from Carter's arms. I wanted to scream, but couldn't; the sound had jammed up somewhere in my esophagus and threatened to choke me. I must have started to run for I felt Carter's fingers digging into my shoulder, holding me. I heard him say something, but the thudding sound of my heart in my ears drowned out his words.

There in the wide doorway stood a monster; something constructed of nightmare and hallucination; something molded haphazardly out of corruption and putrescence. The monster nodded its huge rotting head, and I was afraid that the movement would cause pieces of its flesh to slough off onto the floor.

As a measure of sanity returned to me, Carter's words penetrated my terror. "It's only a costume, Molly. Only a costume."

When his words finally made sense, I could see that what he said was true—a costume, but a very good one. The thumping of my heart slowed, and I began to feel a little bit foolish.

"It looks so real," I said in an awed whisper.

"It's suppose to, my dear," said the monster in a sauve voice. He had a slight British accent that reminded me of Roddy McDowell. "Metronome Pictures invested a princely sum to insure that look of reality."

Still feeling a bit unsteady, I watched as the monster lifted its arms and removed the head.

The face now extending from the monster's body was a face familiar to millions, a darkly-handsome aristocratic face. Since I was a died-in-the-wool horror-film fan, it was certainly familiar to me.

"Raul Del Rio," I said softly.

A charming smile crinkled his face, and he bowed slightly. "At your service. I'm pleased to see that the younger generation knows me."

I smiled back, it was impossible not to. "You're fishing, Mr. Del Rio, you know that you're still the world's 'Best-loved Monster,'" I said, quoting from his own publicity releases. "And I'll have to confess that you've always been a favorite of mine."

He reached out with one of his monster

hands to take mine and raise it to his lips.

He looked at Carter. "It was thoughtful of you to marry a loyal fan of mine, old friend."

Carter laughed heartily and clapped Raul Del Rio on the shoulder. It was more than clear that they were good friends, and I was pleased. Raul Del Rio definitely lived up to his publicity as a witty and charming man. He was in his late thirties, and had been in films since he was a child. A small, rather slender man, he was famous for his many disguises; and his ability to portray "lovable monsters."

"Well," he said, "come in, the pair of you. We mustn't let your new bride stand languishing on the doorstep. Besides, we've arranged a little surprise for you."

I could see Carter tense, and then, with an apparently conscious effort, relax. "Of course, Raul. It's thoughtful of you."

"Not at all, dear boy. It's the least friends can do." Moving with a dancer's grace, he padded ahead of us into a rather dark hallway, the feet of the monster suit making unpleasant squashy sounds on the marble floor. I only had time for a brief glimpse of the entrance hall—it looked terribly formal—before he opened another door, and bowed us into a large living room.

Trying to take in everything at once, I registered a multitude of images: a large friendly-looking room with beamed ceilings, a huge fireplace, jewel-toned Persian rugs; and people, strange, strange people. Dracula was there, and Frankenstein's monster. Music was coming from somewhere, and the Mummy was dancing something that looked like a foxtrot with a fish-belly-white lady with green hair.

They were all there, all the shadowy frightening shapes from the popcorn-smelling darkness of a thousand movie theaters.

Carter looked down at me fondly. "Shut your mouth, dear, and say hello to my friends."

I shut my mouth, and smiled. Now that the initial shock was wearing off, I was touched. These were Carter's friends. All the stars of the horror genre had gathered here to wish him, and me, well in their own inimitable way.

That evening I met the real people behind the screen images that I had admired and that I had been thrilled and chilled by.

But I was tired from the long plane ride from Florida, and the ride in from the airport. Fatigue, plus the drinks that people kept pushing on me, soon had me feeling kind of dizzy. Later, I would remember the evening as I would a dream. It was a dream-like situation anyway. All these famous people milling around—dancing and laughing—and in the center of it all, the man I loved. My husband, Carter Faraday, evidently loved by them, too.

He looked so handsome, so distinguished, standing there among his friends. Once again I wondered why he refused to make pictures any more. Whenever I broached the subject he always froze, shutting me out almost angrily. Most times he was a gentle compassionate man. But during those moments there was a hardness in him, an anger verging on the cruel.

It was almost, I thought, as though he hoped by being cruel to wall me off from that area of his life. I dismissed such flights of fancy scornfully. I didn't know him well enough to make such judgments, but then there were a lot of things that we didn't know about each other. After all, we had only known each other for three weeks.

It was good to see him smile. He smiled too seldom, I thought, as he came toward me now, accompanied by an elderly seemingly indestructible lady with a henna-red frizz of hair and a down-turned mouth. Her eyes were dark and hard as agates. I recognized Emma Boles, famous for playing evil nannies and sinister housekeepers.

Carter introduced us, and she shook my hand, firm and brisk, like a man would.

"Glad to meet you, child," she said, voice equally brisk. "We were beginning to give up hope that Carter would ever come to his senses and act like a regular human being again, though that statement may sound peculiar considering the present surroundings and company."

"Now Emma," Carter said with an indulgent smile, "you'll have Molly thinking that I was a recluse or something."

Emma looked at me with bird-bright eyes. "Is that what you'll think, Molly?"

I smiled at her. "I think he has some very nice friends, who care about him, and want the best for him."

Emma's sudden smile made her hard old face attractive. "That's a pretty sharp young woman you've brought home, Carter."

Carter nodded, and tousled my hair gently. "Yes, she's young, but she's also precocious. I really married her for her mind."

"Hmmm," said Raul, who had strolled up in time to overhear Carter's remark. "A likely story. Anyone who sees Molly will have trouble believing that."

He turned to Carter. "Carter, old friend, I think it's about time for a few words from the bridegroom. I know how you..."

Raul was still speaking, but I didn't hear the rest of his words, because I looked at Carter in that moment. His face had grown white as paper and his body was rigid. He was staring at the wall across the room, and the expression in his eyes sent a chill of apprehension through me.

I followed the direction of his gaze expecting to see, I didn't know what, something terrible. But all I could see was an expanse of cream-colored wall, with the shadows of guests flickering on it like screen images. The shadows were a bit grotesque, but no more so than the living people who made them. I couldn't understand what was wrong.

"Carter," I said softly, tugging at his arm, "what is it? What's wrong, darling?"

At first I thought he wasn't going to answer, that he hadn't even heard me. Then he spoke, his voice low and hoarse. "There, don't you see her?"

"Who?" I said. "Who, Carter?"

"There!"

He pointed and I looked again at the wall. This time I could see what he was talking about. Among the shadows of the guests, or superimposed over them I should say, was another shadow, clearer and darker than the others, unmistakably the shadow of a woman hanging by her neck. You could see the body swaying gently as it swung from the end of a rope.

Cold with sudden fear, I whirled to see who or what was casting the shadow. But there was nothing unusual to be seen, nothing in the path of the light that could cause such an image to be thrown on the wall.

Raul and Emma had now noticed Carter's agitation and they, too, were staring at the image of the hanging woman.

"What is it?" I whispered.

Raul shook his head, but his eyes, when he looked at me, told me better than words that he knew something he would not tell me. One by one the other guests began to notice that something was amiss, and I could hear an undertone of uneasiness creep into their voices. The room slowly became deathly quiet and still as all talk ceased.

Carter and I stood frozen, for different reasons, and Emma took charge.

She clapped her hands and announced in a loud firm voice, "I think it's time we all cleared out and let the newlyweds get some rest."

Almost gratefully, it seemed to me, the guests accepted this suggestion. Their goodbyes and best wishes went almost unnoticed by me. All I could think of was Carter. What was wrong with him? Why was he standing there like that; like a statue or a catatonic?

In what I'm sure was less time than it seemed, we were alone. I looked at the wall again. The shadows, all of them, were gone. Carter still stood without moving, staring at the empty wall as though in a trance, waiting for some hypnotist's signal to awaken him.

I touched his arm. "Carter? Darling, what's wrong? What is it? *Please* tell me!"

He looked around at me with an expression close to horror. He jerked his arm out of my grasp and, almost at a run, headed for the stairs. In a few seconds I heard a door slam on the next floor.

I stared after him, feeling cold and abandoned.

Then I reminded myself that this was Carter, the man I loved, the man I had married. In the short time we had known each other, he had been unfailingly kind, unfailingly thoughtful. There must be something terribly wrong for him to act in such a manner.

I squared my shoulders resolutely and mounted the stairs. It was not until I reached the top that I realized that I didn't even know which room Carter was in. As I reached the top stair, I saw a slender light brown man, dressed in Mao Tse-tung pajamas, standing in the hall. His age was indeterminate and his eyes were expressionless. There was an air of chilly reserve about him, almost as though he disapproved of me on sight.

"Are you...?"

"Yes, Miss." He nodded. "I'm Alexander. Mr. Faraday's in there." He gestured to a door at the end of the hall. "But I'm afraid the door is locked. I took the liberty of putting your things in the room next to his."

Questions and tears rose to clog my throat, but I managed to get the words out, "Thank you, Alexander." I gestured helplessly, and some of the reserve melted from his eyes.

"I know that you don't understand. This must seem very strange to you, but when you know more about all that has happened to Mr. Faraday...," he said compassionately. "He'll be fine in the morning, you'll see. You have a good night's rest."

I looked at him through a mist of tears. Clearly, he believed that my husband had locked himself in for the night. Didn't he realize that this was our honeymoon, and this was our first night home? I certainly didn't intend to spend the night by myself.

I lifted my chin. "I'll just see if I can get him to answer."

Alexander shrugged his narrow shoulders, and smiled at me with a small shake of his head.

Head high, I marched down the hall to the door he had indicated and rapped on it. Once. Twice. There was no answer. I knocked again, louder, and called out, "Carter, it's me, Molly. Let me in!"

Finally he answered, but his voice sounded muffled and strange. "Go away, Molly. Go away. I'll see you in the morning. Just go away."

With the harsh sound of those words ringing in my ears, I stalked stiffly past Alexander's compassionate gaze and into the next room where I threw myself across the bed, and gave way in a flood of tears.

A nagging question plagued me: What other surprises were there in store for a bride who had only known her husband three weeks?

Chapter Two

Of course, in some ways I had known Carter Faraday much longer than three weeks. I had seen every movie he ever made. I had read countless articles in newspapers and magazines about him. I had vicariously suffered with him when his first wife, Nedra Neal, died in an accident during the making of their last film; but, of course, the man I knew was a fictional being, constructed out of newsprint and film strips and my own vivid imagination.

It might seem strange to some that a teenage girl should have a crush on a horror-film star, but Carter Faraday wasn't just *any* horror-film star. In the first place he was young, or relatively so, and incredibly handsome, with a compelling quality about him that made it easy to believe that it would be a simple matter for him to dominate others. With his looks, personality and acting ability, he could have starred in other types of movies. In fact, the fan magazines were constantly printing articles with captions like "Why Carter Faraday Chooses to Do Horror Flicks!" Such articles worried the question endlessly, when the simple answer was that Carter *liked* to do horror films. He liked to perform in character roles, and in films out of the genre they always wanted to cast him as the handsome hero who always gets the girl.

I was fourteen when I saw my first Carter Faraday movie, "Drops of Water," and from that moment on I was lost.

So it was not surprising, when eight years later I came face to face with my idol, that I fell in love with the *real* Carter Faraday. The astonishing thing was that he fell in love with me.

I was twenty-two years old and my father had just died, after a lingering painful illness. We had been very close, my father and I, since my mother had died when I was very small. "Pops," as I called him, had raised and looked after me.

The long tortured months of his illness, and finally his death, left me emotionally and physically exhausted. My Aunt Bunnie, Father's sister, insisted that I get away for a few weeks so that I could pull myself back together. "Some place different, some place where you won't be reminded of home."

I had always wanted to go on a Caribbean cruise, but I was hesitant about going alone so Aunt Bunnie offered to go with me. She took care of all the arrangements, and in a few days we were on a plane for San Juan, Puerto Rico, where we would board the cruise ship.

I still felt depressed and tired, but being on the plane with other people, having to make light conversation, deciding between coffee, tea or milk, slowly began to bring me out of myself.

We arrived in San Juan early on a Saturday morning and took a tour of the island. It was early May, past the height of the tourist season, and the weather was quite warm especially at mid-day, yet it wasn't unpleasantly hot. The island of Puerto Rico was much more beautiful than I had imagined. I was impressed by the efficient grace of El Morro, the ancient grey stone fort guarding the entrance to the harbor, and the awesome jungle beauty of El Yungue, the rain forest.

By the time we boarded the ship I was tired again, but in a healthy rather than a depressing way.

The ship was very beautiful. It looked very much like the cruise ships I'd seen in the movies. I remembered Bette Davis on the deck of such a ship in "Now Voyager." Bette had found romance on the high seas, but I was only looking for a little rest and relaxation so that I could become a human being again.

Although, I must confess, the thought of a shipboard romance did cross my mind. I had been so tied down those last few months that I had had no time for anything but my father. Now I considered a little wistfully the various entertainments promised by the cruise brochures: dancing in the cabaret on the top deck, nights ashore on tropic islands. These weren't the type of things a girl could enjoy doing alone, or even with Aunt Bunnie. However, I had been warned by friends that most of the people taking these cruises were married couples and/or older couples, and single women. All those stories about great shipboard romances were exaggerated.

I soon found out that the stories weren't *all* exaggerated.

We had asked for the late dinner seating, as Aunt Bunnie had assured me that was when the "interesting" people dined. We were asked if we wished to sit alone or with other people and Bunnie, thinking other people would be good for me, opted for that. We were assigned Table Fifty-Eight and, after getting our things stowed away in the surprisingly spacious cabin that first afternoon, we went in to dinner.

I could hardly believe my eyes when our waiter, young and brisk in his short jacket and dark trousers, escorted us to our table. For there, almost hidden behind the huge menu, was a very familiar face. A moment passed while I made the mental transition from screen-face to real-life face. It was that exciting moment that occurs when you see someone famous, someone whom you have only seen on film, in the flesh. Usually there are differences to take into consideration—perhaps they are older, or taller, or fatter than they look on the screen—but not Carter Faraday. He stood as the waiter seated us across the table from him and, yes, he was just as tall as I had thought, just as broad-shouldered, just as handsome.

I pinched Bunnie's arm. "Bunnie," I said in a husky whisper, "do you know who that is?"

Bunnie squinted nearsightedly. "No. But he's certainly handsome, I'll have to say that for him, whoever he is."

"*That* is Carter Faraday, the actor, and he's sitting at *our* table!"

In an instant I was reduced to the palpitating teenager who used to sit in dark theaters, dreaming vague romantic dreams as I watched this man's image on the screen. I clutched Bunnie's arm until she gave me a sharp elbow jab.

"I think I remember now," she said, disgustingly calm. "Isn't he the one you used to have pictures of pasted all over your room? Not so many years ago, I might add."

"Yes," I whispered, afraid to say more. He might just disappear. In a moment I said, "Now just be calm, Bunnie. Pretend you're used to this sort of thing, don't blow your cool."

She snorted, but I didn't pay any attention. I was too busy wondering if I had combed my hair, and if my lipstick was on straight. It was really ridiculous, I knew, but the sight of Carter Faraday had completely undone me.

There was another man at the table, an older man, but I was later ashamed to admit that I never even saw him at the time.

I didn't remember afterward what I ate that first evening, or what had been said at dinner. I did remember that Carter had been polite. We introduced ourselves, and I controlled myself to the extent that I did not gush all over him. I only admitted that I was a fan of fantasy and horror films, and that I admired his work. Later, Bunnie told me I had been vibrating like a tuning fork all the while.

Later, in our stateroom, Bunnie remarked, "So that's your famous idol, your dream man. I can't say he's much of a conversationalist, or maybe I just bored him."

I found myself rushing to his defense. "You just don't understand, Bunnie. He's suffered a terrible tragedy. His wife died under really awful circumstances and, according to the magazine articles, he's still mourning her." A sudden thought struck me. "You know, I'll bet that's why he's on this cruise!"

"Why is that?" Bunnie looked confused.

"To try and forget, of course."

Bunnie sighed and threw up her hands. "Dear God, girl, but you're an incurable romantic! Well, at least he seems to have taken your mind off your problems."

And with that, we went to bed.

By the next night, at dinner, Carter's reserve had broken down a little and I felt that he really began to notice me. The older man at our table turned out to be a Mr. Harker, a widower, who paid charming old-world court to Bunnie, which left me free to concentrate on Carter.

Carter was traveling with his manager, Alf Martin, which explained the empty seat at our table. According to Carter, his manager would miss most of the meals as he suffered from near-terminal sea-sickness.

Within the next few days, Carter and I became warm friends. That is, on his side we were friends. On my side, I was hopelessly in love. I found him intelligent, sensitive, and charming, and he must have found some good traits in me. Otherwise, why would he have been so willing to spend so much time in my company?

There were one or two incidents that made me aware of another side to his nature, a dark and melancholy side; but perversely, that only made him more attractive to me. After all, he was a man whose natural environment was comprised of strangeness and mystery. In addition, he had sustained a great personal loss.

One evening a few nights later he really frightened me. We had gone to see a film in the ship's theater. It was titled "The Cold Winds of November." I had been anxious to see it for some time as it starred my favorite actress, Lila Clair, and Carter wanted to see it because the director, Jules Larson, was a friend of his.

The little theater was cool, almost chilly in fact, with the air-conditioning up high. But Carter put his arm around my shoulders, and I felt warm and happy and cherished.

When the picture came on it gripped my interest immediately, and I almost forgot about Carter, until he suddenly pulled his arm roughly from around my shoulders.

I noticed this fact, but only peripherally, as the scene on the screen at that moment was very compelling. The heroine, played beautifully by Lila Clair, had just stumbled upon the body of her sister, hanging from the limb of a willow tree in their garden. It was both a frightening and a poignant scene, all misty and pastel, with the body of the dead girl swinging gently as the wind stirred the willow leaves and branches.

I wasn't certain just when I realized that something was not quite right with Carter, but gradually I noticed that there was something odd about him. I turned to look at him.

He was rigid as stone and, when I timidly touched his hand, almost as cold.

"Carter?" I whispered. "Carter, what's wrong?"

He did not change expression, or show by any sign that he even heard me. I put my hand on his arm, and it was unyielding, the muscles hard. He seemed to be in some sort of trance, his eyes fixed with a terrible intensity on the screen.

I glanced around in some embarrassment; but there were only a few people in the theater, and they all seemed engrossed in the movie.

Helplessly, I could only sit and wait. The scene in the film now changed to one in a grand ballroom, all grace and light and gay with music. Carter finally stirred. He shuddered, shook his head sharply as though awakening from sleep, and turned a dazed look on me.

"I don't believe I care to see the rest," he said brusquely. "I suddenly have a severe headache. I'll see you at dinner, Molly."

With that he got up and walked out, leaving me sitting there nonplussed and not a little angry. With bad temper I settled down to watch the rest of the movie, determined to enjoy it. I resolved that at dinner I would be distantly polite.

However, at dinner, Carter was his usual considerate charming self. He offered no explanation. And I was fearful of asking any questions, afraid he would rebuff me.

It was almost as if the incident had not occurred.

Looking for Carter the next day, I found him on deck deep in conversation with a stocky dark-haired man about fifty years old. The man had a beautiful tan and a long face mostly obscured by huge dark glasses. They were sitting side by side in deck chairs. At my approach both men got to their feet.

"Molly!" Carter said, smiling. "This is my business manager, Alf Martin. I told you about him. Alf, this is Molly."

"Well, well!" Alf Martin's smile flashed whitely against his tan. "I have been hearing quite a bit about you, Molly. I have indeed."

I could see that Carter had a strange expression on his face, half annoyed, half pleased.

"Now, Alf," he began, but the other man interrupted him.

"No, no, there's no need to deny it, my boy. Let's face it, you've talked of little else since that first night at dinner."

I didn't dare look at Carter, but I was immensely gratified. So Carter was not as cool as he had seemed. He *did* have an interest in me!

"And you're the mysterious Alf Martin," I said. "I had about begun to think that you really didn't exist, that Carter had just made you up."

Alf Martin laughed heartily, then picked up my hand and gave it a friendly squeeze.

"No, no, I'm real enough, it's just my stomach that's not real. And if you don't mind, my dear, let's sit down again. Standing only seems to make it worse."

Carter pulled up another deck chair and we all settled down under the hot sun.

"You really aren't feeling any better?" I asked Alf Martin.

He shook his head. "Not a great deal. But I decided that since I feel rotten no matter what I do, I might as well feel rotten up here on deck."

Carter laughed. "Don't you believe it, Molly. He was afraid he would lose that sun-lamp tan of his."

"You're darned right," Alf said. "It would certainly look funny to come back from a Caribbean cruise paler than when I left. People would talk."

"Have you seen the ship's doctor?" I asked. "I understand that he could give you some kind of a shot..."

Alf waved a hand deprecatingly. "Tried that. The little pills, too. Nothing works. I'm a hopeless case."

Carter sat up suddenly, patting his pockets. "Damn, I forgot my cigarettes. Be back in a minute."

I watched him walk away, and my heart felt like a big spongy marshmallow. He was so darned handsome!

"You like Carter, don't you? I mean, really like him?"

Alf's voice was grave and, when I faced around, I saw that he had taken off the dark glasses. His eyes were as blue as Paul Newman's. For some reason, his question didn't embarrass me.

"Yes, Alf," I replied. "Yes, I like him very much."

He smiled broadly. "Well, for what it's worth, I think he feels the same way about you, although he may never get around to admitting it to you." He slipped the glasses back on.

There was a lengthy silence while I digested this. "But why?" I said in dismay.

He shrugged. "Carter's a rather strange man. He's always been a bit of a loner—moody, unpredictable—but since the death of his wife, he's been almost a recluse. I had to do a lot of fast talking to persuade him to take this trip. Then I had to come along, just to make sure he did come. I was afraid he would seal himself away in that weird mansion of his forever, like those aging hermits you read about..." He shook his head again. "But I was right to insist on this trip, it's done him the proverbial world of good. You're the living proof of that fact. I haven't seen him so alive to the world around him in months."

"Alf," I said, "I have a feeling you're telling me all of this for a reason, that you're leading up to something."

He looked startled, then broke into a pleased grin. "You're smart, Molly, as well as beautiful. Good! And you're right, I do have a reason. I guess that I was hoping that after hearing some of the background, you wouldn't... well, that you wouldn't stop being his friend if he acted a little...well, shall we say a little unusual once in a while?"

His glasses were off again, and his eyes were two question marks.

Fleetingly, I thought of the incident in the movie, then pushed it out of my mind. After all, it hadn't been all that terrible.

I smiled at him. "I'm a faithful friend by nature, Alf. I'm also a spooky-movie fan, and have been hopelessly in love with Carter Faraday since I was fourteen and saw 'Drops of Water.' Give up his friendship? Not a chance!"

At that moment Carter returned with his cigarettes. Our conversation ended, but I could tell by Alf's expression that he was highly pleased. Well, so was I. I had been told in so many words that Carter was pretty darned taken with me.

By the middle of the second week, I knew without a doubt that Carter was in love with me. He never came right out and said so, but I knew it deep in some hidden place. I also knew that he wanted to make love to me, and it was probably a good thing that he was the perfect gentleman because I wouldn't have even tried to resist him. We were at that rather painful stage in a relationship when you can't stay away from the one you love, and it's impossible to touch one another.

We were one day away from the docking back in San Juan when Alf sat us both down in their cabin. He served us each a large Pina Collada and told us, bluntly, that we ought to get married.

I didn't dare look at Carter, for fear I would see rejection in his eyes. There was a crashing silence.

"I mean it, for God's sake!" Alf said explosively. "Here you both are, mooning around like a love-sick Romeo and Juliet, when there's nothing to keep you apart."

Carter finally cleared his throat. "Juliet might be apt for Molly here, but I'm afraid I'm a little long in the tooth for the part of Romeo. After all, I'm... well, I'm old enough to be her father."

I looked at him, all my yearning love in my eyes. "You are not! You couldn't possibly be old enough to be my father because I am really a five-hundred-year-old witch."

We both burst out laughing and fell into one another's arms. No more was said about the difference in ages, or any other differences that might exist.

We were married in San Juan, with Alf Martin and Bunnie as witnesses. Bunnie, in auntly fashion, cried all the way through the ceremony. However, she hadn't been opposed to the marriage. She thought I was a very lucky girl.

We honeymooned for a too-short week in a wonderful old hotel that had been a convent three hundred years ago. Carter was wonderful—tender, compassionate and patient. I felt that I had known him for a hundred years at least.

And I had no misgivings, none whatsoever.

Chapter Three

The morning following my arrival at Trollhaugen, I was awakened by a gentle rolling motion and, for a few minutes, I thought I was still on the cruise ship. I sighed luxuriously, snuggling deeper into the bed. Then I heard a voice speaking my name.

Memories of the previous night surged back and my eyes popped open.

Carter stood looking down at me, his hand on my shoulder. "Wake up, sleepy-head. I've brought your breakfast."

He indicated a large tray on the table beside the bed. It was crowded with silver plate covers and it smelled heavenly. In a ruby crystal vase stood one white rose.

Carter smiled lovingly at me as if last night had not happened at all. He was his usual thoughtful charming self, and I began to wonder if I had dreamed the happenings of the evening before. I was very puzzled by his attitude, but it seemed to me that nothing would be gained by making an issue of it now. I remembered how he had behaved on board ship after the theater episode.

So I let him prop the bed tray across my knees. Bacon and scrambled eggs, orange juice, toasted English muffins, marmalade, and freshly brewed coffee were revealed as I removed the plate covers.

Carter had a companion tray and he joined me.

"Alexander?" I asked, nodding to the tray.

"Yes, Alexander."

"Whatever else he might be, he's a great cook."

"I don't know what I would do without Alexander."

When we were finished Carter said, "After you're dressed, I want to show you the house. You certainly didn't get to see much of it last night."

"That's wonderful, darling!" I pushed the empty tray aside. "I feel like the lady of a manor house."

"And so you are," he replied, ruffling my hair. "My fair lady of the manor house."

He looked so sweet and handsome, so loving, that I could not equate him with the man who had stood frozen in horror in the living room last night, the man who had told me to go away when I knocked on his bedroom door.

I wanted desperately to ask him why he had acted so, why he had withdrawn himself from me but I couldn't bring myself to do it. I told myself that I didn't want to spoil his mood yet I was really afraid of what he might say. It was easier to go along with the moment, and that was exactly what I did.

The house was marvelous, more charming

and whimsical than I had dared imagine last night. There were secret panels and portraits of men with forbidding visages whose eyes followed you no matter where you stood in the room. There were odd little crooks and crannies in many of the rooms, often filled with strange statuary. On the walls I noticed several blown-up stills from some of the more memorable scenes in Carter's movies.

Nowhere did I see a picture of Nedra Neal.

There was a charming little music room, light with sunshine and soft with nostalgia, that contained a lovely little spinet and, to my delight, a harp that sometimes played by itself. Carter refused to tell me the secret of how it worked.

When we had completed the grand tour, I turned to him. "It's like an enchanted castle. I really half expected to find a sleeping beauty in one of the upper rooms."

For just a moment, a strange expression crossed his face and a cold finger seemed to brush my spine. But in a second he was himself again, and I was half convinced I had imagined it.

"I have one more room to show you," he said, guiding me down the hall by the elbow. "It's on this, the first floor. I saved it for last. This house was built by a writer, you know. He installed some of the illusions, and I have added to them."

"What kind of a writer?"

"Science fiction and fantasy—mostly

fantasy—I understand. He lived here for twenty years or more. In fact, he died here when a very old man."

Carter paused before a door at the end of the hall just off the large living room where we'd been last night. "This is the room I wanted you to see, Molly. The Chapel."

With a dramatic flourish he swung open the heavy door.

Inside was a huge room with a vaulted ceiling. There was a raised stage, or dais, at one end. High arched windows were paned with stained glass that threw lovely rainbow patterns on the mosaic floor.

"It's beautiful, simply beautiful!" I exclaimed. "But what's it for?"

Although Carter had called it 'The Chapel', there was no indication of any religious influence in the decor, and the stained-glass windows depicted abstract images instead of portraits of saints. However, there were a large number of folding chairs stacked against one wall.

"I suppose you could call it a theater. We call it 'The Chapel' because it reminds people of a church. This is where our little group meets, Molly."

I turned to him questioningly and he hit his forehead with the heel of his hand. "I forgot! You don't know about the group yet." He hugged me. "There are so many things I have to tell you, Molly, so very many things I have to share with you."

Several minutes passed while he kissed me thoroughly as we stood in a pool of lucent light from one of the tall windows.

"Now," I said, when I could breathe normally again, "what's all this about a group?"

"Well, we call it the 'Club Macabre'. The group is made up of mutual friends who are actors or otherwise involved in the making of horror films. You met some of them last night. Some have retired, some are still working. We get together every two weeks or so to perform scenes from our favorite horror films or plays, strictly for our own amusement." He laughed. "It's a busman's holiday sort of thing but, of course, actors are notorious hams, never happy unless they're on."

I was enchanted. "It sounds like great fun, darling. Do I get to watch?"

"Of course. We might even let you participate." He pretended to consider. "Let's see now. You can be the virgin bride. Or the innocent maiden."

He laughed again and hugged me to him. At that moment Alexander appeared in the Chapel doorway. He was wearing tight black trousers, knee-high boots, and a fitted black shirt of Western design. The shirt was open almost to the waist, exposing a muscular hairy chest. The image was so different from the way I had seen him last night that I gaped at him.

"Miss Emma Boles on the line, Mr. Faraday."

Carter nodded. "I'll take it in here, Alexander."

Alexander left the room, returning a moment later carrying a white phone which he plugged into an outlet in the baseboard and handed to Carter. Then he left quietly.

Carter said into the phone, "Hello, Emma. Yes, we're fine. No, of course not. You and Monica come on over and help yourselves. You can show Molly the costumes while you're at it. I've just been telling her about our club and she is fascinated."

I could hear the rumble of Emma's voice even from where I stood. Finally Carter said goodbye, hung up the telephone and turned to me.

"Emma and Monica are coming over this afternoon to pick up some costumes for a party they're going to. They can show you the props and costumes we use for the club performances. I think you'll get a kick out of it. I'm going to be busy with Alf anyway. We have some business to attend to."

I stood on tiptoe and kissed his earlobe. "Fine, darling! It will do you good to be away from me for a little while. That way, you'll appreciate me more when you see me again."

He answered that remark with a playful swat on the fanny. As we walked out of the room together, I realized that in just a short time he had made me forget entirely about the events of last night. I resolved that soon I was going to have to talk to him about it though. I didn't want any secrets between us, and I didn't want to carry around resentment within myself. Resentment has a way of turning into something nasty. I wanted to give him a chance to explain; but how could I, when he wouldn't mention it, and I couldn't seem to bring up the subject at all?

Emma Boles and Monica Vili turned up precisely at two, just as I had begun to unpack my things. Emma was wearing a pair of aggressively-purple flares, a green T-shirt covered with sequins, and a hideous pink snood tied in a bow on top of her head. She was unbelievable. I had to shield my eyes when Alexander ushered them in.

Monica, better known to horror-film fans as the "Snake Lady," evidently liked to maintain her screen image in her private life. She was wearing basic black. Black jersey, black pants and black shoes. The one note of color was an enameled bracelet on one arm in the form of a snake. It climbed up her arm from elbow to shoulder in a sinuous jeweled spiral that was exotically beautiful. I had only glimpsed Monica briefly at last night's welcoming party and was curious about her. She was quite lovely in her pale expressionless way. In the movies she always wore a long slinky-looking black gown, and had a long, muscular-looking python coiled around her neck.

I suddenly realized that I was staring and greeted my guests cordially, if belatedly.

Emma gave me a friendly cuff on the shoulder. "Well! You look bright-eyed enough this morning. You look as if you've had a good rest."

She beamed at me like a friendly bulldog. I suddenly had the feeling that, if I should mention the business of the hanging shadow of last night, she would pretend that she didn't know what I was talking about.

I shrugged off the feeling and smiled. "Yes, I feel fine this morning, Emma."

"Well then." She rubbed her hands together briskly. "Shall we get to work?"

Monica nodded and smiled, and a transformation took place with the smile. Her whole face lit up. She looked like a young girl and I found myself wondering just how old she was. Emma must have noticed my look of surprise.

"Shakes you up a little, doesn't it?" she said. "She doesn't look like the same girl."

I laughed uneasily. "Monica, I've never seen you smile on the screen, come to think of it. I'll have to confess, you *do* look different."

Her smile widened. "In the kind of movies I make, the cast doesn't smile a whole lot. It would be bad for the image."

I turned to Emma. "I guess you'd better lead the way, you know this place better than I do."

She started down the hall, striding along in a rolling gait, like a sailor. "That'll soon change. You'll feel right at home here before very long, Molly."

She led us into the Chapel, where the afternoon sun sifted through the stained-glass windows forming puddles of rich color on the floor, and back to a door behind the stage.

When she flicked on the light, I drew in my breath sharply. It was wonderfully spooky. Costumes hung on neat racks. There were opulent garments of velvet and brocade, rich with jewels and furs; and strange conglomerations of rags and tatters that looked as if they had been exhumed from a mummy's tomb. On one rack there hung what appeared to be the limp body of a fish man, complete with fins and scales. I could practically smell the sea. On another, hung a strange many-armed creature that looked as if it might have arrived recently from the sands of Mars.

The walls were draped with masks of all shapes and sizes. There were even some full heads. One was particularly creepy—dark green, with bulging eyes and tentacles. I recognized it from one of my favorite pictures.

"Marvelous!" I cried happily.

Emma cuffed me on the shoulder. "Good girl! A real afficionado."

Monica was already busy rummaging through a huge wooden chest that looked as if it might have been stolen from Captain Hook.

"I know it's in here," she said plaintively. "I saw it just last month when we were doing 'Mehitable.'"

I walked over to her. "What are you looking for, Monica?"

She raised a heavy velvet cape and set it aside. "A marvelous costume! No one at the party will recognize me in it."

Finally she brought up a pile of blue fabric and white ruffles, then a blonde wig with long sausage curls.

"I'm going as Miss Muffet," she announced happily, holding the dress up in front of her. "I'm going to change my style completely."

I grinned. "You're right about that. Will it fit?"

"Tell you in a minute." She bundled the costume up in her arms and disappeared into one of the small dressing alcoves along one side of the room.

"And now for me," said Emma, throwing open the lid of still another large chest. "I really haven't made up my mind to anything in particular. I thought I'd just browse until something strikes my fancy."

After a moment's rummaging, she suddenly lifted a garment from the chest, a jewel-red cascade of sequins and velvet. For a moment she stood frozen staring at the dress with the strangest expression on her face.

I felt a little prickle of cold touch my spine. I knew instinctively who that dress had belonged to.

"That belonged to Nedra, didn't it?" I asked in a not-quite-steady voice.

Emma dropped the garment with a startled sound and whirled on me. If I had been in a different mood, I might have been amused by her surprised look.

"Why, yes, it did. But how did you know that?"

I shrugged. "I just knew somehow—the way you froze suddenly—your expression."

She looked uncomfortable. "I was surprised, that's all, Molly. It caught me unawares. I didn't expect to see anything of Nedra's here, after all the..."

She stopped abruptly, and I had the feeling that she believed she had said too much. "After all, it has been two years," she finished lamely.

"Emma," I said quietly, "that wasn't what you were going to say, was it?"

She looked at me obliquely. "Molly, you're a darned sight too perceptive. What I was going to say wasn't all that important. I don't know why I didn't just go ahead and say it.

"After Nedra died, Carter took all her things away. All the costumes she had used, all her personal things. That's all. That's why I was surprised to find this one still here."

"Oh," I said. "He got rid of all her things? Gave them away or something?"

"I didn't say that. I don't know what he did with them, but they disappeared at any rate."

On sudden impulse, I touched her arm. "Emma, would you please tell me about Nedra? I mean, I can't ask Carter. He never talks about her and I have the feeling that he doesn't want to discuss her or the past. He has built a wall around the subject."

Emma waved a hand, as if brushing away the question. "Don't fret about it, Molly. Nedra's dead and gone and there is no point in bringing it up. It won't serve any useful purpose."

She leaned down, pushed the garment deep into the chest out of sight, then closed the lid.

I felt, not for the first time, both jealous and intrigued by Nedra. I couldn't admit it to Emma; but in some deep crevice of my soul I felt that, dead though she might be, she was still a very real rival to me even if it was only through Carter's memory of her.

"It would help me," I said, as cooly as I could.

"It's not just idle curiosity on my part. I think that if I understood, if I *knew* what had happened, I would be able to understand Carter when he..."

This time I was the one who broke off in mid-sentence.

Emma smiled, a dry little smile touched with irony. Or was it malice? "When he what, Molly?"

"When something happens like what happened last night," I blurted out, beginning to grow a little angry now. I hurried on, "You and the others... you're his good friends. Don't tell me that you haven't noticed that sometimes Carter acts, well, strange is the only way I can think to put it. And I think it all has something to do with Nedra's death!"

Emma sighed, and patted my arm in an unexpectedly motherly gesture.

"Molly, Molly," she said chidingly. "Well, all right, if you insist. I suppose you do have a right to know and, as you say, you can hardly ask Carter about it. I doubt he would tell you anything, anyway. Come on, offer me a cup of Irish coffee in that pretty little breakfast room, and I'll tell you what I know."

Chapter Four

"How do you like it?"

Monica popped out from between the curtains, drawing them closed behind her so that they made a backdrop for her pose.

She looked totally different. The blonde wig did something strange, but flattering, to her face so that she looked ethereal and saintly; a lovely, Dresden-like Bo-Peep.

"Fantastic!" I said.

Emma nodded her approval. "You'll knock 'em dead, dearie."

Monica glanced down and gathered the material in at the waist of the dress, pulling it away from her body. "Too big, though. It'll have to be taken in."

"There's a sewing machine." Emma walked over to what appeared to be a small cabinet and opened it. "See, it folds out."

"Oh, good! I'll get right to work on it."

Emma said casually, "We're going to have a cup of coffee, Monica. How about you?"

The other woman shook her head. "I don't think so. I'll stay and alter this, if you don't mind. I don't have a sewing machine at home."

Although I liked Monica, I was just as happy she wasn't going to join us. I suspected that Emma would probably be less reticent with just me as an audience.

Emma and I went into the breakfast room.

As we stood in the doorway, Emma beamed her approval. "Love it. Just like a forest glade."

I had to agree that it was, in a way. A small octagonal room, it seemed attached to the side of the house like a bubble, with windows on all sides. The walls, around the windows, were papered with a lovely soft moss-green paper. The filmy curtains were a pale lemon yellow, and running all around the room, under the windows, was a narrow ledge holding a miscellany of plants in pots. Graceful Boston ferns hung in planters from each angle of the room. Other plants sat about the room in holders. The room, in fact, was almost overrun with plants.

In the center of the room was a yellow wrought-iron-and-glass table with matching chairs. Emma and I sat as I rang for Alexander. I hoped that Emma wouldn't notice how unaccustomed I was to that sort of thing. Ringing a bell and having someone come to do my bidding was a pretty exotic experience.

Alexander popped up with what seemed to me superhuman speed and took our order.

"Now," I said firmly, "tell me about Nedra. What she was like, what happened, everything."

Emma's hard old face softened. "All right, Molly. I'll tell you what I can, what I remember, but I lay no claim to knowing everything.

"First of all, Nedra was beautiful, stunningly beautiful. She was dark and sultry, like one of those early movie vamps, with a strange kind of vulnerability that showed through now and then. She was tiny. Very small-boned and delicate."

I drew my arms and legs close to my body and sat there feeling terribly large, robust and athletic.

"She and Carter were crazy about each other from the start, I guess. It was a real storybook sort of thing. They were always together. You seldom saw one without the other. Although each of them had been stars before they met, after they were married they would only work in pictures in which they could appear together."

I felt a twinge of jealousy. Did Carter love me like that? Would he *ever* love me like that? Of course a love as intense as that could be smothering....

Emma was going on, "Like I said, it was a fairy-tale story. They had everything: money, fame, love.

"Then Carter was approached to do a picture called 'The Wanderer Out of Time'. It was a beautiful story, a sort of twist on the 'Flying Dutchman' or 'The Wandering Jew'. Metronome Pictures was going to put a lot of money in it, it was going to be produced and directed by Sam Eastlake, and there was a wonderful part in it for Carter. But there was one problem... Eastlake didn't want Nedra in the picture."

"Why not?" I asked, astonished. "She was a big star. Why *didn't* he want her, for heaven's sake?"

Emma looked away from me. "I don't know, not for sure, but rumor had it that he was panting after Nedra before she married Carter and that she had turned him down."

"That seems unreasonable. To turn down an actress for a part just because she said 'no' to you?"

Emma looked uncomfortable, and for a moment I was afraid she wasn't going on. Just then Alexander came into the room with our coffee. Emma waited until he was gone before she spoke again. "Well, there was a *little* more to it than that, Molly. I understand she made Eastlake look foolish. He's a vain man. She hurt his pride and evidently he had a long memory.

"Anyway, they wanted Carter to do the picture, but he wouldn't, not without Nedra. A Mexican stand-off, as they say."

"So what finally happened?"

Emma took a swallow of her coffee. "For awhile that's the way things stood. Carter wouldn't give an inch and neither would the director. Then, suddenly, just like that, Sam Eastlake capitulated. Said he'd been wrong, no hard feelings, and so forth."

I shook my head sharply. "I'm puzzled. I've read that Sam Eastlake is a tough director, a taskmaster, but very straight and honest. This sure doesn't sound like it!"

Emma's gaze avoided mine. "Well, I suppose

he had his reasons but, if so, he never told anyone what they were."

I sensed somehow that Emma *knew* what they were, but for some reason refused to tell me. I also felt that nothing would be gained by being too pushy at this point. She might just refuse to say anything more.

So I said, "What then?"

"Then they started work on the picture. By this time, with all the hassle and everything, Carter didn't really want to do it. He had bad vibes about it. But he was committed and, now, so was Nedra. So he really couldn't back out.

"The picture started and for a time everything went along just fine. I saw some of the original footage, before they locked it away, and it was great. It would have been box office, I'm sure."

"What do you mean, *locked* it away?"

Emma shrugged. "Just that. After the accident, Carter bought up every frame of film and had it locked away in his bank vault. You see, he didn't want the footage used...ever. It was too painful to him."

"I know the film was never released, but it was never even finished? By anyone else, I mean?"

Emma shook her head. "Not to this day, Molly, although periodically someone digs up the subject and talks about doing it. Nothing ever happens."

"About what happened to Nedra," I said hesitantly. "I don't want to be gruesome, but I do need to know what really happened."

Emma chug-a-lugged the rest of her coffee

and elevated her eyebrows. "What really happened? There was a lot of controversy about that, many conflicting stories. All I can give you are the details as *I* know them.

"I was on the set that day. I was in a picture that was shooting on a nearby lot, and I dropped around between set-ups to see how they were coming along on Carter's picture.

"It was the hanging scene." Emma's voice grew noticeably softer. "Nedra had been rigged into a harness and a neck brace, and was in her place in what was supposed to be the crumbling tower of an ancient castle. According to the story line, Carter, as Lord Malcolm, stood looking up from the courtyard below. He was supposed to see the silhouettes of Nedra, as Lady Jane, and Raul, as Sinistre, struggling in a lighted tower window. Then he was to see Sinistre hang Lady Jane by the neck to a ceiling beam. Malcolm and the others watching in the courtyard were supposed to be transfixed in shock, as the shadow of Lady Jane slowly swung back and forth in the window.

"Then Lord Malcolm was supposed to run up the stairs, finally reaching Lady Jane just in time, just before she dies. He cuts her down, and she lives. The question in the mind of the audience being, is she really alive? Did he really get to her in time? Or is she actually dead, parodying some ghastly semblance of life?

"As you may or may not know, a movie is shot in bits and pieces, usually out of sequence. The hanging bit, intercut with the reaction shots of Carter in the courtyard, was to be shot separately, with the following shots of Carter rescuing her to be done later. They didn't want Nedra hanging from the neck brace for too long at a time.

"Well, they shot the first frames of the scene. It was perfect, only one take. The director yelled cut, and the grips moved in to help Nedra down off the beam. I was standing alongside Carter by then, watching the scene, so I saw what he saw.

"The window was still lighted. We saw the hanging shadow of Nedra, and the shadows of the grips as they reached up to take her down. Carter noticed something wrong before I did, maybe it was because Nedra's figure looked so limp in the arms of the grips. Anyway, he was running before it dawned on me that anything was amiss.

"When I finally realized that something was wrong, I tried to follow him but, by that time, many people were milling around and things were close to panic. I kept asking what was wrong and finally one of the extras, who had been up close to Nedra and was now trying to push her way out of the crowd, told me.

"'Nedra's dead,' she said. She looked ill. 'Her neck's broken.'

"'How?' was all I could manage.

"The girl didn't know. In fact, that was the question everyone was soon asking. How could it have happened?

"I saw them bringing Nedra's body out of the tower set. Carter walked beside her, holding her hand in his. One look at his face and I had to look away.

"And that's about all I know for sure, Molly. The papers came out with stories about the 'tragic and mysterious death of Nedra Neal.' The studio put a tight lid on the story and no one, who really knew anything, would talk about it. The police called it an accident and, of course, no charges were ever filed against anyone. The official story they finally gave out was that the harness was defective. Or rather, the neck brace. It had broken, you see, and Nedra had strangled to death before they got her down.

"The rest you pretty well know. Carter went into seclusion, refused for the longest time to see even his friends, refused to do any more pictures. Finally we managed to get through to him, and get him part way back into the real world. At least he agreed to holding the club meetings again. But it took you to finish the job, Molly. You know, we're all very grateful to you for that."

Her words were kind, but there was a strange expression in her eyes. I didn't quite know what to say. I was saved from saying anything by the entrance of Monica, carrying the Bo-Peep costume under one arm.

"Well," she said with some satisfaction, "I got it done, Emma. We'd better go, I have that three-o'clock hair appointment."

Emma nodded and pushed back her chair. "Molly, we'll be seeing you Friday. That's the regular night for the club meeting."

I smiled, but I was a little piqued by her bland assurance that the meeting would go on as usual, that my being in the house would change nothing. But that was being petty. There was no reason why my being there should change their club meetings. Besides, I was looking forward to seeing their re-enactments of old horror movies.

I saw them both to the door, we said our goodbyes, and I walked with them down to the bottom of the steps where I stood watching them drive away.

I really don't know what it was that caught my attention. I don't think it was a noise, but for some reason I looked up.

When I saw the thing on the roof staring down at me, I couldn't move. Even when I realized what was happening, I stood frozen.

The face of the figure on the roof was hairy and hardly human, a wolf-face. I could even see hairy arms and paws as it strained the heavy cornice stone immediately above my head. I could see the stone moving and I knew that in another instant it would crash down upon my head. But my feet seemed to have a horrible will of their own and I could not force them to move. I saw the stone tear loose and somehow, in that last second, I jumped clumsily to one side, almost falling.

The stone made a terrible sound as it struck the walk, shattering into several pieces, and I was sick at the thought of what would have happened if I had not looked up at that exact moment. I wanted to vomit and my skin felt cold and clammy.

I literally staggered back into the house. Alexander was not in sight. Shakily, I made my way to my room and into the bathroom. I washed my face in cold water and lay down on the bed. My head felt mushy with thoughts that I didn't want to face.

Just what was it I had seen, or who? There was no one in the house except Alexander, and I wasn't even sure he was there. I had seen Emma and Monica drive away and Carter had been gone for hours.

What had it been, up there on the roof? And then, the most frightening thought of all. Why had it tried to kill me?

Chapter Five

The room was dark, except for a single slanting ray of blood-red light that entered through a high narrow window.

The light illuminated, almost like a spotlight, the pale waxen face of the man in the box. He was dressed in a black high-necked shirt and his slender long-fingered hands were crossed upon his breast.

From the heavy gold chain around his neck hung a huge medallion, embossed with runes. His face looked both noble and sinister in repose.

Now, to the right of the coffin, a door opened and a young woman entered. She was tall slender and golden-haired. Her face was the face of an innocent, or a saint. She approached the coffin and stood motionless in the light, which bathed her hair with sanguine tones.

It was fantastic! I nearly forgot that I was watching the enactment of a scene, it was so real. The costumes, the lighting, the acting, were all excellent. It was difficult for me to remember that the man in the coffin was not the evil vampire, Count Vladov, but Roger St.

James, the most recent inheritor of Lugosi's mantle, and that the ethereal maiden was really Monica.

I hugged Carter's arm to my side in the dark as the heavy black and gold curtains slid slowly across the front of the small stage. A man rose up out of the audience. He had a large wolfman head in his hands, which he now placed over his own head.

I felt my muscles go tense. Carter grunted and pried my fingers loose from his arm.

"I don't mind your being passionate," he whispered, "but you're bruising my arm, Molly."

Then he looked at me more closely, and evidently noticed something unusual in my expression.

"Molly, what is it? What's wrong?"

I didn't know quite how to answer him. I hadn't told him about the incident of the falling cornice stone. That is, I had told him about nearly being hit by it, but not about seeing the wolfman on the roof pushing it off. It sounded melodramatic, even to me, and I couldn't help questioning what I had seen or what I thought I had seen.

Also, Clive Martel, the actor who specialized in wolfman roles—the man I'd just seen donning the wolf-head—was a good friend of Carter's. If I told Carter, it was bound to sound like I was accusing Clive of trying to kill me, and that was just plain ridiculous. Underneath it all, I just had a gut-level feeling that it was better not to mention the wolfman on the roof.

So I smiled, and released my grip on Carter's

arm. "I guess I'm just excited. It all looks pretty real."

"It does, doesn't it?" He smiled proudly. "There is some high-powered, and high-priced, acting talent here, you know. You're seeing it all for free. I hope you appreciate that!"

I nodded. "I know. And I do appreciate it."

The curtains were parting again. This time the scene was a forest glade, or perhaps I should say a forest glade with overtones of schizophrenia. Everything was subtly distorted and out of focus. It looked like a forest scene in a bizarre dream.

Into this scene glided a slender figure in grey, with pearly white skin and floating silver hair, that seemed to move on some unearthly breeze. As this eerie figure flitted between tree trunks, a high-pitched keening sound could be heard: a strange, almost, but not quite, music.

Suddenly the figure stopped center stage. The wolfman, dressed in a futuristic tunic and tight-fitting trousers, could be seen creeping in from the back of the stage.

"This is a scene from 'Planet of the Lost'," Carter whispered in my ear. "Vanda Evers is doing the role she did in the movie, Etherelda, the Mist Woman. Have you seen the film, Molly?"

I shook my head. "No, I missed it."

"I thought you saw all the fantasy and horror flicks?"

"I do, most of them, but that one never did come around. But I wish I had seen it. It must have been unusual."

"It was. Perhaps too unusual for public taste.

The picture didn't do at all well. That's probably why it never played in your neighborhood."

"What was the story line?"

"It's supposed to take place a hundred years or so in the future. A time when mankind has shipped off all its unwanted human garbage to other planets. All the physical misfits have been banished to the planet Eleria, where they have interbred, bringing into existence strange mutations of the human form."

At that moment, a third figure joined the two already on the stage. It seemed to be a male; slender, with a narrow face and a high bulging forehead. The figure appeared to be nude except for a soft-looking pale green fuzz.

"That's Raul," whispered Carter. "He's playing Fadua, Etherelda's lover."

The two males were circling each other now in a slow formalized fight. It was almost like a ballet.

Although all three were very good in their roles, it was Raul who stood out. He had a wonderful talent for using his body to express feeling and emotion. When, in the part of Fadua, he lay writhing on the floor of the stage in a simulation of death, it was uncannily and uncomfortably real.

As the curtains swept across the stage and the lights came up, I released the breath that I did not realize I had been holding. I saw Carter shaking his head, smiling.

"That Raul. As often as I've watched him perform, I never get used to it. He's really something else."

"He's very good," I agreed. "But I know someone else just as good." I took a deep breath. "Don't you ever miss it, Carter?"

The smile left his face. The skin around his eyes and mouth tightened. Then he sighed and gave me a wry grin. "I would be lying, Molly, if I said I didn't miss it...sometimes."

I squeezed his arm. "Then why don't you act again? I mean, there is no reason..."

He silenced me by simply placing his large hand firmly but gently over my mouth.

"Molly, that is a subject I'd rather not talk about, if you don't mind."

His words were a rebuff. I felt a combination of embarrassment and anger, embarrassment for being made to feel gauche and anger that there should be something between us we could not talk about. Also, anger that he should hush me like a naughty child.

I pulled away from him, got to my feet and hurried past him through the Chapel door.

I almost collided head-on with Alexander, who was approaching down the hall. He was wearing a flowing caftan and a turban. He nodded politely. "Dinner is set up in the main dining room."

I gave him a half-hearted glare, but went along in the direction of the dining room.

The room was beautifully arranged: the china and crystal sparkled against the dignified gleam of the silver; a long buffet table, at the side of the room, gracefully displayed a bountiful repast on its polished surface.

The others began drifting in within a few minutes. First came Emma, wiping her face with what appeared to be a large red bandanna.

"Whew!" she said, sighing noisily. "Guess I'm getting old. Can't take it like I once could."

Behind her walked Raul with Vanda Evers clinging to his arm.

"You?" Raul said, laughing. "You'll never grow old, Emma, my dear. You're too preserved in sheer wickedness."

Emma guffawed and turned to him, aiming a mock punch at him.

"Look who's talking! You were so real in that part tonight that I am more than ever convinced the *real* you is a creature from outer space, just pretending to be human."

Vanda's tinkling laughter climbed over the sound of their voices as I stood watching them, suddenly feeling very much the outsider. Past them, I saw Carter come into the room. His glance met mine and passed on, deliberately cool.

I was weighing whether I should go to him and try to make amends for my abrupt departure in the Chapel when Raul saw me. He disengaged Vanda's arm from his and came toward me. He was smiling widely and appeared delighted to see me. He placed both his hands on my shoulders and, pulling me close, gave me a kiss on the cheek.

"Little Molly," he said in that precise voice. "Lovely as a single rose in the midst of this motley collection of freaks."

His breath smelled of mint and his lips were fresh and cool. Little Molly indeed, I thought. In my heels I stood an inch taller than he.

His hands still on my shoulders, head tilted to one side, he studied me intently, then shook his head. "You're a beautiful creature, Molly. I don't know why you didn't wait for me instead of marrying Carter!"

I answered his smile, yet I felt somehow ill at ease. Despite his warm words and his actions, I instinctively felt there was something about this situation that didn't ring true. There were undertones here, several layers of meaning in what Raul and the others were saying. Were they trying to spare me from something?

"Come on," he said, taking my arm. "You'll sit next to me, my dear."

He led me away toward the buffet, just as the rest of the group entered the room.

No one seemed to notice that I looked a bit startled when Clive Martel took the seat on the other side of me. I gave him a half-hearted smile and turned to my dinner with a sudden loss of appetite.

Not overly reassured by the presence of Raul on my other side, I glanced around for Carter. He was seated at the far end of the table, deep in conversation with Abner Snare. Abner was a small wizened-looking individual who, before horror films, had made a career out of playing crafty shopkeepers and sniveling office clerks. He had had, even in youth, a strange little-old-man face and, on the screen, a fawning servile manner that made him a pleasure to hate.

In reality he seemed to be a very nice shy sort of man, with a rather old-fashioned courtliness about him. For some reason, I was glad that Carter was talking to him.

"How did you like my performance?" said a voice in my ear.

It was Clive Martel, on my left. I faced him and found his brown eyes friendly and inquisitive. He appeared to really want to know my answer.

I said, "Fine. I loved it."

Clive was younger than some of the others, about thirty, with a thatch of tawny hair on his head and a matching blond vee on his chest where his shirt collar opened. He was nice but undistinguished looking, sort of like a younger better-looking Lon Chaney, Jr.

Looking into his guileless eyes and pleasant face, I simply couldn't believe that the wolfman on the roof had been Clive. He wasn't that good an actor and any one of them would have had access to the costumes. But more important than that, what possible reason could Clive have to want to harm me?

Gazing around the room, I couldn't think of anyone with a reason to harm me. I caught Carter's glance. He winked at me and I smiled back. No use holding a grudge.

Carter turned back to resume his conversation with Abner.

"Molly?" It was Roger St. James, who was sitting across from me. Roger was a sinisterly handsome man who appeared to be in his early fifties. His long sardonic face with the thin aquiline noise and aristocratic eyebrows was well-known by the movie fans of two generations.

"How did you like my scene?"

"I adored it. You were magnificently horrid."

He laughed. "Horrid! Good heavens, have I finally come down to that?"

"I meant it in the nicest way."

Monica, who was sitting next to him, asked him something just then and I turned my attention again to my dinner. The food was very good. Not for the first time I wondered how Alexander, all by himself, managed to do it and still have time to change costumes so often.

With some food and wine inside me, and the light conversation going on around me, I began feeling better. Things were going to be all right, I just knew they were. Whatever Carter's problem was, we would cope with it. We would solve it together.

The falling cornice stone? The wolfman on the roof? Well, maybe I would eventually find an explanation for those things.

It was late when the last guest left. Carter and I stood in the driveway, waving them away in the chilly after-midnight air. Emma was the last to go, waving jauntily to us as she spun the wheel of her little yellow sports car. We stood for a moment watching her car's tail lights vanish down the drive.

Carter said with a huge yawn, "It's been a great evening, hasn't it, Molly?"

"A wonderful evening, darling."

I took his arm and we turned back toward the house.

The front of Trollhaugen was brightly lit by concealed directed lighting. As we started to mount the steps, one of the lights suddenly went out leaving the right side of the front of the house, with its truncated tower, dark.

I jumped, startled by the sudden change, and I could feel Carter's arm stiffen under my hand. I drew in a sharp breath, which made a funny sobbing sound, because centered in the brightly lighted tower window was a sharp black shadow—the shadow of a woman moving slowly back and forth. I could even see the shadow of the rope around her neck.

We stood there for what seemed an eternity but at most it could only have been a few seconds.

I heard a muffled groan from Carter. Before I could turn to him, he had disengaged his arm roughly from my grip and plunged into the house.

I called his name and ran in after him. The inside of the hall was also dark. That was a little frightening, since I knew we had left the lights on. I could see nothing; and heard nothing but the drumming of Carter's footsteps as he hurried toward the tower room.

It took me several minutes of fumbling to find the light switch. My mind was a jumble of confusion.

"Alexander?" I shouted. "Where are you?"

The sound of my voice echoed and re-echoed down the hall, but there was no response. Not knowing what else to do, not really wanting to, I hurried after Carter in the direction of the tower room.

Chapter Six

The lights in the stairwell leading up to the tower room had been made to resemble torches set in brackets on the walls. The light they cast was dim and yellow, like torchlight, and it made the stairwell look like something out of a "Tower of London" movie set.

I had the weird feeling that everything I was experiencing was a movie scene. That it had all been staged, and I was an unwilling performer in a drama for which I had not even been allowed to read the script.

My footsteps echoed hollowly as I ran up the stairs. The sound of my own breathing was a rushing noise in my ears.

Finally I reached the heavy wooden door at the top, the door to the tower room. It was firmly closed and I could hear no sound but the thudding of my own heart.

Tentatively, I called Carter's name. There was still no sound. My hand trembled badly as I reached for the huge, iron latch that held the door closed. I grasped the cold iron and pulled. The door slowly opened with a faint squeaking noise.

Bright light splashed out and washed over my feet. Someone had replaced the dim fake torch bulb with a white high-wattage bulb. Every detail in the room stood out sharp and clear.

The room was completely empty. There was no hanging woman and, what was more important, no Carter.

I sagged against the door frame, feeling out of breath and confused and even more frightened than before. It was quite impossible!

Carter had rushed into the house only a few seconds before I had. He had gone up the stairs, I had heard his footsteps going up, and I had followed right behind him. There was no other way out of the tower room, no way other than the stairs. Carter *had* to be here! And yet, he wasn't.

I made an attempt to pull myself together and looked carefully around the room again.

"Remember," I told myself aloud, hoping that the sound of my own voice would be somehow reassuring, "this is a trick house. Maybe there's a secret passage!"

It finally dawned on me that since this was a tower, and there was nothing on the other side of the walls except air, secret passages in the walls would be impossible.

I studied the room itself more carefully. There was a large heavily carved chest of drawers, an immense velvet-covered throne-like chair, a low rough-hewn table, and that was all. A large faded tapestry covered about half of the curved wall and a smallish dark rug lay across the center of the floor.

I pulled the tapestry away from the wall; behind it was solid, unmovable stone. The large chest was empty and the table was too small to conceal anything. I even lifted a corner of the rug and found the same solid uncommunicative stone.

Feeling as if all the strength and spirit had been drained out of me, I left the room turning out the light before I closed the door. The only thing that made much sense was the light. It would have been necessary to have a lot of light to cast the shadow of the hanging woman so we could see it from below.

The stairwell was chilly now, as I trudged downward touching the cold stone wall from time to time for support.

Once out of the stairwell, there was an almost palpable silence. I tried calling again for Alexander but received no answer.

I went directly to Carter's room. His door was locked but I could hear movement inside.

I knocked. "Carter?" I called in a choked voice. The sounds of movement stopped, but I received no response. I called again without much hope.

There were tears in my throat and in my voice. I could not, and did not care to, hold them back. All my beautiful dreams were curling up and dying around me. I felt all alone and hurt.

Finally, knowing he wasn't going to answer me, I turned away toward my own room. It was going to be a repetition of the first night.

But it was worse, much worse. That night was the longest of my life. I thought of telephoning Bunnie, just to hear the sound of a familiar voice, but it was late here and it would be long after midnight in the East. Besides, Bunnie could always tell when something was wrong with me. I really didn't feel up to discussing my personal problems but I was afraid I didn't have the strength to dissemble.

Finally, I put on my nightgown and stretched out on the bed. Sometimes, when things are bad for me, I can escape into sleep but not this night. The house, Trollhaugen, which I was coming to love, had all at once grown frightening to me. I could hear groanings and creakings that I hadn't been aware of before. A strong wind had come up and, if I hadn't felt so miserable, I would have laughed. It was so like a scene in one of those movies. You know the kind I mean. The young woman alone in an empty mansion; strange sounds in the night and the wind, or a storm, always blowing outside.

I lay sleepless for a long while, listening to the sounds. Then I began to get angry. Just what was going on here? Where the devil was Alexander? Why didn't he answer when I called? What was a grown man, my husband, doing locked in his room like a frightened child? I was beginning to feel very mistreated and being mistreated always makes me furious.

I got up, put on my robe and went to have another try at Carter's door.

There was no sound at all inside his room now and there was still no answer to my repeated knocking.

Angrier than ever, I jerked the belt of my

robe tight. How did I know he was even still in there?

The wind made a sudden surge against the window at the end of the hall and something clunked downstairs. Was the house locked up tight? Before this night I had never given it a thought, but tonight I knew that I would never sleep unless I knew that all the doors and windows were locked and bolted.

I started with the downstairs. The front door was unlocked. I bolted it firmly against the wind. In the small breakfast room I found a window open. The wind was tearing at the leaves of the Creeping Charlie hanging in front of it. I closed the window and picked up the fallen leaves.

The deserted Chapel looked spooky and smelled of melted candle wax. I forced myself to go through it anyway, even the dressing area. There was no one there, of course, only the rows of empty costumes looking like skins shed by some exotic forms of life and the jars of cold cream on the dressing tables.

I found a small cleristory window open and closed it.

The kitchen was warm and snug. The back door was locked. I made myself some hot chocolate, poured it into a mug and drank it before continuing my checking of the house.

The sun room, with its clusters of plants, was humid and empty. The maid's room, which Alexander used, was empty also. For a moment I studied it intently hoping to get a clue to the man's personality. But the room was as austere as an Army barracks, with none of the homey touches that living usually gives to a room.

My solitary trudge almost ended in the music room. Before I ever opened the door, I felt that a window must be open because the sound of the wind was much stronger here. I pushed open the door and, sure enough, the large window across the room was open. Wind was blasting into the room, riffling the sheet music on the spinet and blowing dust over the polished top.

I hurried to the window and pushed it shut, noticing that the wind had become much stronger.

Suddenly, behind me, the harp began to play.

The crystal clear notes cascaded like ice water over my skin. I jumped and whirled around to stare at the instrument.

I felt as if all the blood had been drained out of my head. I watched the harp strings moving rhythmically, as though plucked by invisible fingers. It was all I could do to keep from running screaming from the room.

Even in my paralyzed state, the sound of the music was hauntingly familiar; a sad little melody. I tried to remind myself of what Carter had told me about the harp. It was a trick, a mechanical contrivance. But the question I could not answer was who? Who had turned it on? Carter had called it a "ghost" harp. I shivered uncontrollably.

It took all the nerve I could summon but I reached forward and touched the harp, moving it slightly. The music stopped abruptly, as though I'd thrown a switch.

I fled the music room, gratefully slamming the door after me.

Thoroughly unnerved now, I seriously considered calling a cab and spending the night in a motel. Then I began to get angry again. Why should I let myself be driven out of what was now my own home?

Propelled by righteous anger, I stormed up the stairs and began my rounds of the second floor. The harp was a trick instrument and it worked on some mechanical principle. Perhaps the wind had set it off. That thought brought me some comfort, though not enough to really lift my spirits to any great extent.

I hadn't realized that there were so many bedrooms on the second floor. Besides Carter's and mine, the room I used when he locked me out, there were four more. They were all neatly made up, all quite comfortable and charming, and all the windows were closed. Then I discovered that my first count was wrong. There were five; there was another door at the end of the hall.

I reached for the knob. It turned in my hand, but it would not open. I shook it a little, thinking that it might be stuck, but there was no question about it. The door was locked. I put my ear to the panel and it seemed to me that there was a faint stirring sound inside.

I backed away from it. I had just remembered the story of Bluebeard, his wife, and the locked door. But even without such melodramatics, the house was missing two men, at least as far as I could tell, and I was being confronted with not only one but *two* locked doors.

I returned to my room, locked the door from the inside and got into bed. I didn't know whether it was the walk through the house or the hot chocolate, but in a short time I was asleep. I remember that my dreams were uneasy, something about Bluebeard and a giant harp that played by itself.

I awoke the next morning as the sun sliced through the window and washed over my face. I was fully awake immediately. At once I remembered all that had happened the night before. My anger also returned. This time, I promised myself, there would be no covering up the situation with breakfast in bed and fond husbandly kisses. This time, I would demand to know just what was going on. I had a right to know.

I jumped out of bed and quickly pulled on a pair of pants and a shirt. I washed my face, put on a dash of lipstick and tied back my hair. I felt full of purpose, but I knew that underneath lurked a lot of doubts. A lot of tears were just below the surface.

The wind had died during the night. It was one of those beautiful clear California mornings that I had heard followed such winds. It was as if the sky had been scrubbed clean for the new day. I determined that this would indeed be the start of a new day for Carter, and for myself as well. I would convince him that it was best to be completely honest with me, best to tell me what was wrong.

I knocked briskly on his door. I heard the bed creak but there was no answer. I tried the knob. It was locked.

"Carter!" I called, and pounded on the door with both fists. "If you don't answer me, I'll stand out here and pound all day!"

I guess he must have realized I would, because he answered. His voice was cold and completely emotionless. "Molly, go away. *Please* go away! Leave me alone."

Dismay was a lump of ice in my stomach. "But Carter, I must talk to you! Won't you let me in? Please, darling!"

"Molly," he said in that same hard voice. "You don't understand. I can't talk to you now. Please leave me alone. Just go away."

"Go away." The words might have been stones he was hurling at me; they couldn't have hurt more.

Tears blinded me as I whirled and ran down the stairs, colliding with Alexander at the bottom.

"I'm sorry, Mrs. Faraday," he said, backing a step.

"Where were you last night?" I shouted in a burst of fury. "I called and called for you! You never answered!"

He looked at me without expression, his smooth brown face as inscrutable as any Oriental's. "It was my night off," he said in a strangely gentle voice. "Friday night is always my night off, Molly. When they have the meetings, I fix the buffet, then go."

"Don't call me Molly!" I shouted again, pushing past him.

"Will you be wanting breakfast?" he called after me.

I didn't answer him. I was already ashamed of myself for shouting at him. There was absolutely no reason to vent my anger and frustration on Alexander.

I marched into the study, looked up Alf Martin's office number in the phone book Carter kept in his desk drawer and dialed it. It was Saturday. I hoped his office would be open.

After the phone rang several times, a too-sweet voice announced, "Mr. Martin's office."

In a moment I had Alf on the line but then was at a loss for what to say to him.

"Alf," I finally said, "I've got to talk to you. It's very important."

"Of course, Molly," he said without hesitation. "Come on over to my office. Are you okay to drive?"

"Oh, yes, I'm not that far gone. I'll be right over."

I banged the receiver onto the cradle and ran upstairs taking the steps two at a time. I got my purse and a scarf, then hurried down the stairs and out toward the huge stone garage which was located a short distance behind the house.

I thought I was being completely cool and in command of myself, but I almost leaped out of my skin when I saw the garage doors begin to slide open before I reached it.

It gave me the most awful shivery feeling because, as far as I knew, Carter was in his room and Alexander was also in the house.

There shouldn't have been anyone else around.

Instinctively, I ducked behind the big jacaranda tree just to the right of the garage, scrunching up, hoping I wouldn't be seen.

The door continued to slide back, but no one came out immediately. I had begun to think it was just a malfunction of the doors, when I saw a movement inside in the dimness of the garage. I could see all three cars inside: Carter's two and my little red bug. After a moment a figure emerged from the gloom between my car and Carter's black Mercedes. The figure stepped cautiously out of the garage, and after looking around, moved quickly and quietly around the side of the garage toward the rear of the lot and out of my sight.

It was all I could do to keep from bursting into hysterical laughter. The figure was that of a witch—a traditional Halloween-type witch with a conical hat, straggly hair, and big nose.

She was even carrying a broom!

Chapter Seven

My first thought was: what was Ellie Stovall doing in our garage? Then I reminded myself that it wasn't necessarily Ellie just because she customarily played witch roles. Any member of the club could get to the costumes in the Chapel. The witch was not necessarily Ellie, any more than the wolfman had to be Clive Martel. But whoever it was, what the devil were they doing in the Faraday garage?

I waited a few minutes, behind the jacaranda tree, before I headed toward the open garage door.

I switched on the light inside. Nothing seemed to be wrong or out of place. My little car squatted there looking practical and snug. Everything seemed normal enough.

All the doors to the bug were still locked. I shook my head in puzzlement. Well, no use worrying about any stray witches now. There were more important things to worry about; such as my husband, my marriage and what in the name of all that was holy, or unholy, was going on?

I unlocked the car, got in, and turned on the

ignition. Carter had bought the little car for me a few days ago, when I'd told him that I felt uneasy driving either of those big monsters of his. I always felt pretentious in the back with Alexander chauffeuring me about. The bug started up immediately, with a friendly growl, and I started down the long winding driveway leading to the street that headed out of the Hollywood Hills and into town.

I turned on the car radio, which I always kept tuned to KFAC, and the soothing strains of Rodrigo's *Fantasia para un gentilhombre* filled the little car. I took a deep breath and relaxed a little. Maybe Alf would be able to sort it all out for me, give me a new perspective.

Then the strains of the music died away and the announcer's voice came on. I never heard what he was saying because, at that moment, I attempted to brake lightly for a sharp curve and found I had no brakes.

I have often heard the old expression, "Her heart was in her throat." I didn't know whether or not mine was in my throat, but it certainly wasn't in its usual place!

I felt a cold gut-wrenching twist of fear and had time to wonder if I was going to die before my whole being was involved in an effort to forestall that event.

Thank God I was driving a small car! The bug cornered very well and that undoubtedly helped keep me from plunging over the cliff on my left. That, and the fact that there were no cars coming just then. The street was narrow, two lanes only, but at least I had it all to myself.

Everything seemed to be happening in

super-fast time. My brain felt frozen. I yanked back on the emergency brake. It was loose in my hand. It did no good at all. I was going too fast to try and shift down.

Grimly, I hung onto the wheel and reacted faster than I knew I normally could. I didn't have time to think about the mile or two of upgrade that lay just a short way ahead. I was too involved with the moment. But when I saw it, it looked like a miracle. I knew I was saved. The momentum of the car took it a short way up the incline. Then it rolled back. Still no other cars. Thank God!

Finally the car came to a stop. For a long moment I slumped over the steering wheel, too weak and shaky to get out. After several gasping breaths I pushed open the door and stumbled out.

It was still the same glorious day but I felt chilled through and through. As I stood just outside the car door, trembling with a delayed reaction, I realized that the radio was still playing.

Finally the melody penetrated my scrambled consciousness. It was the same sad little melody that the harp had been playing last night.

Alf Martin's office was in one of the new highrise buildings on Wilshire Boulevard. The building was so elegant, in fact, that I wished I had put on something dressier before leaving Trollhaugen.

His office was just what I would have

expected: thick carpets, heavy expensive furniture, and a busty silver-blonde secretary in a short skirt and low-cut blouse.

I must have looked the way I felt, because the first thing Alf did was pour a stiff drink of brandy into a large glass and insist that I drink it.

"My God," he said, "what happened, Molly?"

I sipped at the warming brandy and tried to pull myself together.

"Had a little trouble with the car," I said, trying to be flippant. Then the whole thing came pouring out, starting with the failure of the brakes and going backwards through the experience last night, to the wolfman on the roof, all the way back to Carter's baffling behavior on the night I first came to Trollhaugen.

"Something is wrong," I said, then started to laugh. After all I had told him that statement struck me as very funny.

Alf smiled, somewhat sadly. "Yes, Molly, I'd say that something is very wrong and maybe part of it has been my fault. I really thought Carter was over this thing, or I never would have encouraged him to marry you."

He got up to pace back and forth behind the desk. Finally he stopped and looked at me. "I don't know how much you know about his wife's death..."

"Carter has never talked to me about it himself. Emma told me what happened, and what she told me is all I know."

He nodded. "Well then, you probably know

most of it. He and Nedra were very close. Her death was a terrible blow, compounded by the fact that he felt he was to blame for the accident."

I leaned forward. "Emma said something like that, but I thought that was just part of his grief at the time."

Alf shrugged. "No, it hung on afterward and he apparently still believes it. You see, Carter is a perfectionist. He always insisted on making his movies as authentic as possible. He never wanted his fans to feel 'cheated', as he put it.

"In the business with Nedra, it was a matter of the harness used in the hanging scene. There were two rigs available, I understand. One was safer than the other but it didn't give the same realistic effect. Carter insisted they use the one providing the most realism. It was safe, too, he had checked it himself. But it was still riskier than the other one. Anything Carter wanted Nedra went along with without question, so they used the harness Carter wanted and Nedra was hung."

Alf raised and lowered his shoulders in a gesture of defeat.

I let out a long sigh. "Poor Carter. What a tragic thing to have happen!"

Alf walked back to his desk, poured himself a shot of brandy and downed it. "Yes, nothing that we, his friends, could say could get the thought out of his head that he was somehow responsible. Even when the police assured him it was simply a freak accident, that no one was actually to blame, it still didn't shake his conviction. It was a terrible time for him."

"It must have been. Emma told me that he went into seclusion and refused to see anyone."

Alf took another drink of brandy. "That's right but Carter is a good man and, because he is, he has good and loyal friends. We didn't give up. Slowly but surely, we began to pull him out of his depression. And when he met you, I figured we were home free. I was positive everything was going to be fine, but now this..."

He waved his hand in a gesture of resignation. "It strikes me there are two possibilities. One is that someone is harassing Carter on purpose, trying to remind him of the past and Nedra, striving to drive him back into that earlier state of depression. The other possibility is that Carter is..."

"Losing his mind," I finished for him. "No, I can't accept that, Alf. Don't forget, I've seen those things, too. We've both seen the shadow of a hanging woman twice. The first time the others did, too, if they will only admit it."

Alf nodded. "I believe you, Molly. But you know how well liked Carter is, both in business and out. Who would hate him enough to do something like this to him?"

An unpleasant thought popped into my mind as Alf said this, but I shook it away, and took another swallow of brandy.

"You will help us?" I said.

He put down the brandy snifter and stepped forward to take my hands in his. His strong, friendly face was serious.

"You know I will, Molly. I'll do all I possibly can. Now, come on, I'll take you home."

The front door of Trollhaugen was locked. As I rummaged in my purse for the key, the door opened. Carter looked out at us. He was pale, but composed, and showed no surprise at seeing Alf with me on the doorstep, although I felt plenty at seeing him open the door.

"Hello, Alf," he said calmly, and then to me, "Darling, I've been wondering where you were. Why didn't you tell me you were going out?"

I felt my mouth fall open in astonishment and glanced around in time to catch Alf giving me a very funny look.

"Where's your car?" Carter asked.

Seeing that I was evidently unable to speak for myself, Alf gave him the answer. "It's in the shop, Carter. Molly came close to having a nasty accident. Her brakes went out as she was coming down the hill."

Carter's face went white. "My God!" he said.

He seized me and held me close. This was the only reaction he had shown that made any kind of sense to me. I clung to him and babbled out how I had been on my way to town, carefully not mentioning why. I also neglected to mention why I had called on Alf for help and not my husband. Under my breath I swore, if he asked that question, I would kick him in the shins, as much as I loved him. Thank God, he didn't ask it.

He finally held me off, his eyes searching my face as if looking for damage. He sighed in relief. "Well, come on, you two, let's not stand out here."

We went into the den, a cozy little room that the original owner had furnished, quite literally, to look like the den of an animal.

Carter smiled at Alf. "Thanks, friend, for taking care of my bride. You don't know how much I appreciate it."

Again Alf gave me one of those searching looks. It was clear that he found Carter's actions at variance with the story I had told him in his office.

It finally dawned on me that there was only one thing to do—bring it all out into the open. Clearly we weren't going to get anywhere as long as Carter pretended that nothing out of the way had happened.

"Carter," I said firmly, taking a grip on myself, "I've told Alf about what has been going on. That's why I was going into town. I think we need help and Alf was the only person I could think of who might be able to help us."

Carter turned his back on us and stood looking out the window. He kept his face turned away as he said in a neutral voice, "Need help? In what way do we need help, Molly? Alf, I'm sorry that Molly has wasted your time like this."

He swung around to face us. His expression was perfectly composed. He could have been talking about the weather. "Molly dear I know you've been a little nervous and upset, but I can't imagine what you've been telling Alf here."

An icy fist cramped my stomach and I felt my face grow stiff with anger. I said as calmly as I could manage, "Carter, you know very well what I'm talking about. Now that Alf knows, too, why not drop all this pretense and admit it? Perhaps he can help us."

Carter shook his head. "Alf, I'm truly sorry. I don't know what on earth she's talking about."

He turned to me with a look of grave concern that made me angrier still. "Molly, darling...maybe it's the strange surroundings and Trollhaugen. Everybody knows it's haunted." His short laugh was not very convincing. "And on top of that, this near accident. It's understandable you would be upset. But don't worry, it'll be all right."

Hot tears flooded my eyes. With one hopeless nearly-blinded look at Alf, I whirled and ran from the room.

I hurried upstairs to my room. Hating myself for showing such weakness, I wondered what Alf must be thinking. What in the world was I going to do now? It seemed so hopeless as long as Carter blandly ignored any hint that all was not right with his little world here in Trollhaugen. Was he losing his mind as Alf had hinted? Worse, was I losing mine?

I scrubbed the tears out of my eyes and doused my face with cold water. Well, I wasn't going to run away. I wasn't giving up yet. I was determined to have it out with Carter. Somehow, some way, I had to make him listen to me. I had to get him to admit there was something wrong, get him to tell me why he was so upset.

I went out of the room and to the top of the stairs where I could see the front door. There was no use in confronting Carter with Alf present; it would only be a repeat of the scene I had just gone through, and I knew I couldn't take that again. I could hear the rumble of their voices from the den.

Alf didn't stay very long. After about another ten minutes had passed, he left. Carter escorting him to the door. I hurried down the stairs.

When Carter turned away from the front door, I was standing right behind him.

His face, when he saw me there, looked so melancholy and pale I couldn't help wondering how much it had cost him to keep up the facade he had shown to Alf.

"Carter, why did you do that to me?"

"Oh, Molly," he said, gazing at me with such love and desolation in his eyes that I started to cry again. He held out his arms and I rushed into them.

"Molly, Molly," he kept saying over and over. "Forgive me, darling, please forgive me!"

I raised my face. "But why, Carter? Will you tell me why?" He didn't answer immediately, and I went on. "Alf probably thinks I'm crazy, one of those neurotic females who fly into hysterics at the slightest excuse."

"He'll understand some day, Molly."

"But why put me through it? It's not fair!"

Carter pushed me gently away from him and looked down into my eyes. "I know, Molly, I know. I'm being terribly unfair to you. But I have my reasons." He sighed. "It's all so bloody complicated!"

"Does it have something to do with Nedra's death?" I asked softly.

He nodded. "I've never told you about it

because it's nearly impossible for me to talk about it. The psychiatrist told me I have a mental block." He smiled wryly. "I can't seem to talk about it to anyone, not even you, Molly. You see, I believe that it was at least partly my fault that she died. If I hadn't insisted on using that particular harness...."

Carter took his hands away from my shoulders and balled them into fists. The expression on his face was one that made me hurt for him.

I placed my hand gently over his lips. "Emma told me how Nedra died. Then Alf filled me in on some more of it. Both say it wasn't your fault."

Carter tried a smile, but it was ghastly caricature. "That's what the psychiatrist said, too, but it still doesn't keep me from feeling that it was."

I brushed a strand of hair out of my eyes. "But you were over it, at least almost over it, when you met me. Alf says he thought you were doing fine."

"I thought so, too. I was so damned sure! But now something is happening." He gripped my shoulders again. "You saw that hanging shadow, too, didn't you?" His grip was painful and the look in his eyes frightened me. "Didn't you?"

"Of course I did, darling," I assured him hastily. "But why didn't you talk to me about it? Why did you run away and lock yourself into the bedroom?"

He said tightly, "I don't know if you can understand, Molly, but seeing that hanging shadow took me back to the day she died. You can't know what that was like. It was Nedra, Nedra come back to haunt me. I know that sounds crazy but it's what I thought. Then when it happened a second time last night...do you realize, Molly, that the tower room is a near replica to the one erected on the set of that last movie?"

"I know it's bad, darling. I can imagine what it must be like but there's nothing, *nothing* in this world so bad we can't share it!"

Carter pulled me into his arms again and held me so tightly he forced the breath from my body.

"Molly," he said into my hair, "you are the sweetest most loyal wife a man could ever have. I'm very fortunate."

I pulled back. "You're darn right I'm loyal, but don't think for a minute that will keep me from asking for an explanation of why you acted the way you did just now in front of Alf."

The worried look crept back into his face. "Molly, shadows don't just happen by themselves. The only possible explanation is that someone is *making* those shadows. I don't know why they're doing it, but someone is deliberately trying to disturb me and it could be anyone—any one of my friends. Do you understand what I'm saying?"

Suddenly, I did. "You mean Alf. You think it could be Alf? But he's your business manager and your friend. What would he have to gain?"

"They're all my friends but it has to be one of them. It has to be someone with access to the house and someone who knows about Nedra.

Don't you see, I can't, I don't *dare*, let them know this is getting to me."

"Why would anyone want to do this to you, Carter?"

"I haven't the least idea but the fact remains that someone is."

"Couldn't it be a woman?"

"Yes, it could be a woman. The only one I'm sure it *isn't* is you, Molly."

We looked at one another thoughtfully and I decided this was as good a time as any to tell him about my "accidents."

I told him as we walked upstairs, our arms around one another. At the top of the stairs I remembered the locked door. "Carter? One of these bedrooms is locked. Why is that?"

He looked away from me. "That was Nedra's room. I couldn't bear to go in there after she died, so I locked it. I'd wall it over, if I could."

The bitterness in his voice shocked me. "But I heard someone in there! I'm sure of it. There was someone moving around in there last night."

He shook his head firmly. "Impossible, Molly. I don't even know where the key is. That room hasn't been opened since shortly after Nedra's death."

I stared at him doubtfully. He still avoided my gaze. I *knew* I had heard someone, or something, in that room but perhaps now wasn't the time to press it. I didn't want to destroy our re-found rapport, so I hugged Carter as hard as I could with one arm and happily went with him into our bedroom.

Nedra's room could wait until another day.

Chapter Eight

It was only later, as I lay at his side, that the questions returned to plague me. I *had* heard someone in that room. I was positive of that. If the door had been locked since Nedra's death, and if the key was lost, who had it been? And how had they gotten in?

Was someone really trying to drive Carter back into a state of depression, and perhaps madness?

I rose up on one elbow and gazed down into his face. Relaxed now in sleep, the tense lines around his mouth had smoothed out and his features looked young and peaceful.

The thought that had popped into my head in Alf's office surfaced again. What if Carter were staging these incidents himself? It was possible. Disturbed people have been known to do that sort of thing and not remember it later. This thought scurried around in my head like a sharp-clawed feral creature until I forcibly threw it out. No, that wasn't the answer. However short a time I had been with Carter, I knew him. Knew him in the deep intuitive way that it is possible to know someone you love very much. This could not be the answer. I wouldn't let it be!

I carefully slipped out of bed and put on a caftan, moving quietly so as not to waken Carter.

Now that we had talked about it, now that it was out in the open, I felt easier in my mind.

A hard determination was driving me. I was going to get to the bottom of this; whatever it was, this thing that was destroying my husband and tearing at my marriage. And it seemed to me the logical place to start would be in Nedra's room.

I closed the bedroom door gently after me. Carter hadn't stirred once since I got out of bed. I could hear faint sounds coming from downstairs. The hum of a vacuum cleaner told me that Alexander was occupied for the time being.

I walked down the hall to the door at the end and tried the knob. The door was still locked. I pressed my ear to a panel but could hear nothing other than the pulsing of my own blood.

How could I get in? I thought vaguely about wax impressions, and having keys made, but I really didn't know how to go about that. Then, I remembered a technique I'd seen so often on television and in movies. I looked closely at the lock. It appeared to be the same type of lock that is usual on inside doors; the type that opens with a simple skeleton key.

I went quickly back to the bedroom, slid my purse off the dresser and removed one of my credit cards.

A few minutes later I was ready to push open the door of the "mystery room", as I had come to think of it.

My heart was thudding wildly. I felt guilty as the devil. But there was no sound from our bedroom and the hum of the vacuum was still coming from downstairs. Taking a deep breath, I shoved open the door and slipped inside.

I had no idea what I expected to see but it was certainly not what I did see. The room was dark, except for the red glow of a small votive candle set in a red glass. The flame wavered in the draft created by the open door. The soft red light, reminding me of a scene acted out at the Club Macabre meeting, washed over a long white oblong box which was setting on a raised dais above the low table holding the candle.

As the light flickered over the box, I felt an unreasoning surge of fear. It was all I could do not to back out of the room. Then anger rose hot in my throat. It was abundantly clear that Carter had lied to me again. The "mystery room" hadn't been locked all this time!

I fumbled along the wall for the light switch. I wanted to see it all.

No overhead light came on. Instead, wall brackets holding artificial torches like those in the tower stairwell blinked into life.

The room was clean and neat, as only regular cleaning can make a room. Votive candles do burn for a long time, but they need someone to light them and they have to be replaced now and then. I leaned my back against the wall and studied the room carefully.

The first thing my gaze went to was the white box resting on the marble dais. It had a familiar shape; wide at one end, narrow at the other, like an Egyptian sarcophagus. An elaborate gold scroll design was worked into the cover. It was very beautiful, and very eerie, and I would not let myself speculate about what it might possibly contain. I was feeling too hurt to go much past the thought that Carter had lied to me.

I tried to swallow past the lump in my throat. I stared at the huge theater bill that had been framed and placed on a gold and white easel beside the white box. It was an old advertisement for one of Nedra Neal's movies, and Nedra's face stared back at me with huge dark-rimmed eyes. She had a mocking half-smile on her lips, almost as if she were aware of what I was thinking. I shivered as I stared at the picture.

To the left of the dais was a huge canopied four-poster bed with a red velvet coverlet and large fat velvet-covered pillows. The rest of the furnishings looked like something out of an opium dream; ornate, and somehow stifling.

My gaze was inevitably drawn back to the white box. It couldn't be. It simply couldn't be what it looked like!

I had never before experienced the conflict of emotions I felt as I forced myself to walk toward that box. I wanted to know what was in the box, yet I didn't. Maybe nothing, maybe something that would destroy my life with Carter. I had to know, yet my every instinct warned me away from it.

I don't know how long it took me to approach the thing but finally I stood before it.

The lid was hinged and firmly closed with a golden hasp in the form of a snake.

Gingerly, I grasped the snake. It moved easily in my fingers. The box wasn't locked. Even more tentatively, I took hold of the smooth white wood and lifted. Then, with a sudden burst of courage, I flung it open.

I think, if I had not been holding both sides of the coffin, I would have fallen because it was just that—a coffin. Inside lay Nedra. Nedra, as Cleopatra, with shoulder-length black hair and an Egyptian crown upon her head. Nedra, uncorrupted and as beautiful as in life.

My knees started to give way but, as I slid toward the floor, I heard a horrible scream that could only be coming from my own throat. Screaming must have kept me from fainting.

The next thing I knew I was running down the corridor, careening from wall to wall.

I burst into our bedroom. The light was on and Carter was sitting bolt upright in bed.

"My God!" he said. "What was that scream?"

"Carter, Carter!" I babbled. "It's Nedra, in a coffin, there in her room. *Why is she there,* Carter?"

Carter stared at me wildly and leaped from the bed, pushing me aside. He was halfway down the hall before I could collect myself enough to run after him. I reached the door to

Nedra's room just in time to see his frozen figure standing in the middle of the room, and to hear the awful moaning sound coming from his throat. It sounded as if he were choking. Then I saw her...

Hanging from one of the heavy ceiling beams was Nedra's body. Slowly and grotesquely it revolved, swaying gently. It almost seemed as if she were dancing there in the air.

Chapter Nine

Carter pushed past me with such violence that I was thrown against the side of the door. I was vaguely aware of another door slamming after a moment and I belatedly realized what I had done by bringing Carter into this room, in exposing him to this new horror.

I raised my eyes to Nedra's revolving figure but my fear was receding now. At some level of consciousness, I had already registered the fact that this was no human figure but a life-sized doll, the one I'd seen earlier in the casket and had thought was real. Despite the rope around its neck, the face smiled secretively and the shoe-button black eyes stared blankly over my head.

I slumped slowly down into a sitting position against the wall by the door. I felt stunned. My brain, overloaded and overtaxed, did not want to think, only to rest. Yet there were so many questions and no answers.

She had been a small woman, Nedra, I thought, as I watched her likeness swinging there in the center of the room, and very beautiful. Beautiful enough to warp a man's mind with grief? Fascinating enough to cause Carter to build a shrine in this locked room? Was Carter mad? Was I?

There was only one concrete fact that I could cling to. Whoever or whatever had made this room into a shrine to Nedra, it could not have been Carter who had hung the doll up by the neck. I had reached the door only seconds before him. There simply would not have been time.

I was aroused from my stupor by the sound of an indrawn breath. I looked up and saw Alexander standing in the doorway. The expression of shock and horror on his face eliminated any possibility that he had known the secret of this room.

"Mrs. Faraday, what is it? What happened?"

He must really be shaken, I thought wryly. He called me Mrs. Faraday instead of Molly.

He hurried to me and, grasping me by the elbows, helped me to my feet. His usually bland face wore an expression of concern. I noticed for the first time that he was really quite a handsome man.

"Alexander, do you know anything about any of this?" I waved my hand to include the hanging doll and the coffin shrine.

He shook his head vigorously. "I've never been in this room, Mrs. Faraday. When I first came to work here Carter told me that this room was to be kept locked, that I didn't need to clean it. I was forbidden to ever enter it. I don't even have a key."

I nodded. "Then have you ever seen anyone else going or coming from this room?"

He shook his head again. "How could they? The door is always locked. I don't understand this, not any of it."

"You're not alone in that, Alexander," I said, not telling him how *I* had gotten in. "I don't understand it, either."

I simply couldn't get to sleep that night. Alexander had tried to get Carter to open his door, but had finally put down the tray of food he'd brought just outside on the floor.

I made no attempt to talk to Carter. I felt guilty for getting him into that room. I knew how much he had been shaken by the shadow business and I felt that I knew how he must feel now, after being confronted by the hanging effigy of Nedra. I also knew it was useless to try to get through to him now. Eventually he would have to open his door and we would talk about it. Although what good that would do, I didn't know.

After trying reading, a glass of hot milk, and music—none of which succeeded in making me the least bit drowsy—I went into the bathroom for a sleeping pill.

I'm not a pill taker as a rule. I dislike the idea of having to rely on artificial means to sleep; but I still had a few of the pills that the doctor had prescribed for me after my father's death. I took one with a glass of water and, in about a half hour, I was able to drift off into a troubled sleep.

My dreams were by Dali out of Warhol,

directed by Felini. The most vivid of them I will never forget. I was running, panic-stricken, along the upper halls of Trollhaugen—a Trollhaugen distorted and magnified as though seen in a fun-house mirror. I knew that someone or something terrible was chasing me but I didn't know what it was.

As I raced past a huge gold-framed mirror, I glanced behind me and saw a great bat-winged shape hovering over me near the ceiling. I screamed and flung up my arms. As I did so, I looked into the mirror. Fresh horror seized me when I realized I could see only myself in the mirror. The creature with the bat shape had no mirror reflection. Then it was upon me, smothering me with its dark wings and gripping my shoulders painfully with talon-like hands. I felt sharp teeth at my throat, then the hot slimy trickle of my own blood running down my neck. A tremendous surge of panic gave me superhuman strength and I flung up my arms to break the monster's grip...and awoke.

I awoke to a horror greater than the dream. My flailing arms had struck something where nothing should be. My eyes could make out a darker shape against the darkness of the room and I was conscious of someone breathing. Instinctively, I grabbed my pillow, flung it at the dark shape and screamed as loudly as I could.

In a moment I heard footsteps running toward the door and the sound of the door being flung open. I kept on screaming. I couldn't seem to stop, although a part of my mind was saying: silly twit, that's enough now; knock it off!

Then the light came on, blinding me, and I could hear the concerned voices of Carter and Alexander as they rushed toward me. I finally managed to close my mouth, shutting off the awful sound. As my eyes became accustomed to the light, I saw the worried look on Carter's face. I gratefully registered the thought that, however great his own problem, he had unlocked his door and come to me when I needed him.

The clamor of their voices, both trying to talk at once, confused me. All I could say was, "A vampire, a vampire!" over and over.

Finally Carter succeeded in quieting Alexander and took my hands. "Molly, calm down. Try to calm yourself. Now tell us what happened?"

I took a steadying breath. "Someone was in here, in this room, standing over my bed."

"We didn't see anyone." He shot a look at Alexander. "Are you certain it wasn't just a dream?"

I shook my head vehemently. "I *had* been dreaming, an awful nightmare. That's what woke me. But when I awoke, there was really something here, it was doing... something to me. I'm not sure what..."

Carter stepped back, his expression still concerned, but I thought I detected a growing doubt beneath his concern.

Then Alexander pointed, "Look, Carter, Look at her neck."

I gazed at Alexander. He looked both puzzled and horrified, the most expression I'd ever seen on his face. Now Carter was staring at my neck, too. An equally strange look came over his face as he reached a hand out and touched a finger to my throat. He drew it away and held it up so that we all could see.

It was covered with blood.

Things became a little hazy for awhile after that. I remember a doctor coming, doing something to my throat and sticking a needle into my arm. After that I remembered nothing for several hours. When I awoke Carter was sitting on the bed beside me. I touched my throat and found a small bandage on the right side of my neck.

Everything came back to me with a rush. I gasped and grabbed Carter's hand in a compulsively tight grip.

He said tenderly, "It's all right, darling. It's all right now."

"There *was* someone here," I whispered. "Wasn't there?"

He nodded soberly. "Yes, Molly, and whoever it was meant you no good. The wound in your throat was made with some sort of sharp two-pronged instrument."

"Like a vampire's bite," I said with indrawn breath.

"Yes," he said. "At least it was *meant* to look like a vampire's bite."

I shuddered.

Carter squeezed my hand and looked deep

into my eyes. "Molly, don't worry. I'm going to stop this thing. Trying to frighten me is one thing, but when they try to hurt you..."

I smiled weakly. "But who is 'they', Carter, and how will you stop them?"

His gaze remained steady. "I don't know, yet. But I'll find a way."

"We could go to the police."

He shook his head. "And tell them what? That I see shadows of hanging women? That you have been threatened by a werewolf, a witch and a vampire?" He shook his head again. "Think what the newspapers and scandal magazines would make of such a story. A horror-film star plagued by creatures from his own films!" His smile was bitter. "It would be a madhouse and, in the confusion, whoever is doing all these things would likely get away. No, I'll have to do it myself."

It was my turn to shake my head. "Oh, no, you won't, you male chauvinist! *We'll* do it!"

He hesitated for a moment, then his eyes began to glow, and he smiled slowly. "Darling Molly. All right, *we'll* do it. Now, the first thing, I'd like to get them all together, all the club members. We just had our usual twice-monthly meeting, so I thought perhaps a party. We haven't given one yet and it would be perfectly natural for newlyweds to throw a party for friends."

"That sounds good, then what?"

He shrugged. "I'm not quite sure, I haven't worked out the details yet. Maybe we stage a scene of our own."

"What do you mean?"

"Well...maybe I'll script a scene or two depicting all the things that have been happening, then watch our audience carefully to see if anyone reacts."

"It sounds as if it might be worth a try. But are you all that sure it's one of the club members?"

"It must be. It almost has to be, Molly."

"Which one do you think it might be, Carter? You know them all well. Which one could do a thing like this?"

"That's just it. I can't imagine *any* of them doing such a thing. Yet, I know it has to be one of them. First of all, it has to be someone who knew about Nedra and how she died." His face grew very still and sad. "And second, it has to be someone who has access to the Chapel and the costumes, someone who can come and go without arousing too much suspicion."

"Help me to sit up," I said, trying to lift my shoulders off the pillow.

Carter propped the second pillow under my head and shoulders. I raised my face to kiss him on the cheek.

"But I'm still puzzled," I said. "I never saw anyone come into the house before either of the times I was attacked. The doorbell didn't ring and I'm pretty sure Alexander didn't let anyone in. The only times I've seen any of the group here are when Emma and Monica came over to look through the costumes, the night you brought me home to Trollhaugen, and on the night the club met."

"That doesn't necessarily mean anything. You see, they all have keys to the house. I gave them each one so they could get into the Chapel any time they wished. The key unlocks the side door that leads through the dressing rooms. I wanted the Chapel to be available to them for rehearsing. In a way, it's a sort of club room, a meeting place."

"Then any of them can come into Trollhaugen at any time. If they parked away from the house, we might never know they're here."

"That's right," Carter said. "It seemed like a good idea in the beginning. Since we've been married, I just never thought about changing it... until now."

"You're going to ask for the keys back?"

He nodded, sighing heavily. "It may result in some wounded feelings and I realize that there is nothing to prevent them from having had copies made. Still, if they all turn in their keys, and later we catch one of them using a key..."

"I see what you mean." I felt suddenly cold. I tried to smile brightly. "Well then, we'll have a party!"

"This weekend. I'll get Alexander started on it tonight." He looked at me gravely. "I'm only sorry that your first party at Trollhaugen won't be under different circumstances, Molly."

"Tomorrow you can tell Alexander," I said, taking a firm grip on his hand. "Tonight your somewhat frightened bride needs you at her side."

Carter smiled, that tender loving smile that so warmed my heart. Still, it did not wholly dissolve the feeling of apprehension that had me in its grip.

Chapter Ten

Trollhaugen really looked festive. Alexander had cleaned and waxed and polished until the house fairly shone. The scents of lemon wax and various flowers filled every room.

The food was being catered and the caterer was providing two people to serve. Everything was under control. If the situation had been different, I would have been looking forward to my first real party in my new home. Even under the circumstances, I could not help being swept up in the sense of excitement that planning a party brings, for periods of time almost forgetting the purpose of the party.

Throughout the arrangements, Carter remained preoccupied and withdrawn. Every night before going to sleep beside him, I prayed that the party would bring things to a head; that he would finally learn who was doing these things to us and why.

On the night of the party, I took special care with my dress and makeup; and if I do say so myself, I looked pretty good. Good enough, anyway, so that Carter snapped out of his preoccupation long enough to notice. He smiled and kissed me soundly, almost undoing all my artistic efforts before the party even began.

The guests were magnificent! They did Trollhaugen justice. Emma was done up in royal blue satin, two-inch eyelashes and exotic feathers. Raul wore a tuxedo, made from odd pieces of blue denim which managed to combine elegance with a rag-bag effect. Monica was stunning in black velvet beautifully embroidered with a snake which coiled up her belly and between her breasts.

The remaining guests arrived so fast I couldn't take time to study each individual outfit. They were all chatting and smiling. It was very difficult for me to believe that one of these nice pleasant people hated either Carter or myself enough to try to destroy us.

The music from the multi-plex filled the rooms and the hallways in competition with the laughter and chatter of the party.

The waiter and waitress that the caterer had provided mingled with the guests, carrying trays of drinks and canapes. Carter and I mingled also. I found myself watching faces carefully, noticing gestures, unobtrusively eavesdropping.

We had set one room, the large living room, aside for dancing. As I entered my arm was taken by Clive Martell, who looked nothing at all like a werewolf in a beautifully-patterned silk dinner jacket and a delicately ruffled shirt.

"May I?" he asked, and before I could demur, he swept me onto the floor, which was already occupied by Abner Snare and Ellie Stoval. Abner, in a conservative dinner jacket, looked sensible and ordinary. Ellie, in beige lace, looked delicate and ladylike. They both nodded and smiled at us, as Clive led me onto the floor.

I gazed up into Clive's open honest face and tried to think how I could phrase the question I wanted to ask him. There was just no way I could think of to inconspicuously work into the conversation. Finally I came right out with it. "Clive, I've been wanting to ask you something."

He looked down at me with nothing more in his face than normal curiosity. "Sure, Molly. What is it?"

"Two weeks ago, on a Tuesday afternoon, were you here at Trollhaugen? I mean, did you come by to borrow a costume, or perhaps rehearse in the Chapel?"

He missed a step, his eyebrows climbing in surprise. "Why, no. The only time I've been here since the night you arrived was last Friday, for the meeting. Why do you ask?"

I found myself smiling apologetically. "Because I saw someone, wearing the wolfman costume, up on the roof that day."

He looked confused. "In the wolfman costume? That's odd, very odd. Are you sure?"

I nodded. "Quite sure."

"Well, I'm afraid it wasn't me, Molly. But who do you suppose it could have been? Maybe one of the others playing a prank on you?"

"Yes," I said, smiling stiffly, remembering how close the cornice stone had come to killing me. "I guess that was it, just somebody playing a prank."

We finished the dance and I excused myself.

I sensed that Clive was telling the truth. Or he was a far better actor than I was willing to give him credit for.

I smiled at Monica and Roger St. James, who were just coming onto the dance floor, and admired Roger's blood-red jacket, which so well complemented Monica's black velvet. The eyes of her snake just matched the red of his jacket.

I encountered Carter in the hall and we exchanged notes. He had talked to Ellie Stoval. He was convinced she was telling the truth when she denied being at Trollhaugen on the day my car brakes failed.

"So that leaves us right back where we started, doesn't it?" I said, and told him what Clive had said.

Carter sighed. He ruffled my hair with a rueful grin. "Chin up, Molly. At least we have more or less elimated two suspects, and the evening has hardly begun."

Suddenly, I became conscious of the sound of the spinet from the music room, the notes barely audible over the dance music coming from the multi-plex. I frowned in thought. I couldn't quite catch the melody, but what I could hear sounded familiar.

I seized Carter's arm. "Come on, let's see who's playing the spinet."

At the open door to the music room Carter and I both stopped short. I because I could now recognize the tune. Carter for reasons of his own. I looked around at him and noticed that his face was quite pale.

"Carter, what is it?" My stomach suddenly

felt hollow. Was he going to retreat from me again?

But he only moved his shoulders in a slight shrug. I could see the muscles of his face tense as he took a deep breath. Then he made a visible effort to relax. "It's all right, Molly," he said calmly enough. Taking my arm, he led me into the room.

Raul was seated at the spinet, looking graceful and competent, his chin raised slightly, and his slender beautifully-shaped hands moved smoothly over the keyboard. Emma was standing nearby with a drink in her hand. Vanda was sitting across the room in a high-backed chair.

Raul glanced around as we entered. His playing became even better, as if his talent grew with the size of his audience. He had the talent of a professional pianist.

As the sad graceful melody poured out of the spinet, I knew it for the same melody I'd heard twice before. Once in this very room, on the self-playing harp, and once on my car radio after my brakes went out.

I stepped up to the spinet. "Raul, what's the name of that piece?"

He looked up at me and smiled charmingly. I was very conscious that both Emma and Vanda were watching me intently. Vanda's face had gone completely blank and Emma's eyes had a strange look. I glanced around for Carter. He reached for my hand and squeezed it reassuringly as Raul finished the number with a soft closing chord.

"It's Ravel's *Pavana Pour Une Infante*

Defunte; 'Pavane for a Dead Princess'. Do you like it?"

"Yes, very much," I said feeling uncomfortable under the combined stares of Emma and Vanda. "I've heard it a couple of times recently and wondered what it was."

"It was Nedra's favorite piece of music," Carter said, quickly and harshly. I could feel his hand tighten on mine.

Raul looked surprised. "Why, so it was, Carter. You know, I had completely forgotten that."

Was his expression of surprise a bit contrived? I looked at Emma and Vanda. They seemed to be listening and watching a bit too avidly for this to be the casual exchange of chit-chat it seemed on the surface. I felt very uneasy and wasn't quite sure why, perhaps because of the mention of Nedra?

"It's strange you didn't remember," Carter was saying. "I mean you all spent so much time here with us." He turned to Emma. "Do you remember the piece, Emma?"

Emma smiled, but the smile didn't quite match the glittery look in her eyes. "Remember that *Pavane* was Nedra's favorite? Why, yes, Carter, I remember."

Raul shook his head ruefully. "Well, I'm really sorry, old boy. I shouldn't have played it. Stupid of me." He gestured with graceful hands and his expression was certainly contrite enough this time.

Carter was completely in command of himself. "It's okay, Raul. Don't worry about it. It didn't upset me. I just wondered if you knew, is all. No, don't get up." Raul had started to rise. "Go on with your concert. Molly and I are just playing the dutiful hosts, checking to see if everyone is having a good time."

Carter tucked my arm firmly in his and steered me out of the room.

"What was that all about?" I asked, as soon as we were out of earshot.

"I'm not quite sure. I'll have to think about it. Don't you think it's about time for our little drama?"

I nodded. "Might as well. Who did you get to help out?"

"Ellie and Clive. We've already talked to them. Will you be all right?"

I smiled brightly, despite the fact that about two dozen butterflies had just been released in my stomach.

"Of course, darling. I'm a natural actress, didn't you know that? I just hope there aren't any talent scouts in the audience. They might want to persuade me to leave you for a career in pictures."

Carter chuckled, and patted my hand.

The truth was, however, that I was a bundle of nerves. When Carter had suggested that we stage a skit incorporating the two attacks on me, with me playing the lead part, it had seemed the right thing to do. Now, thinking I would be performing before a group of professionals almost did me in.

At least I was type-cast and needed no special make-up or costumes for the part. I suppose you could say that I had lived the role.

When I entered the Chapel, I could hear

someone moving around in the dressing rooms and thought it must be Ellie or Clive. I could have gone back and chatted, but I wasn't in the mood for light conversation at the moment. I wondered what Carter really expected to learn when we performed the skits. Did he hope that someone would show surprise, or shock? Would someone look guilty? Carter had told me he was going to stand against the wall to one side of the audience so he could watch their faces while the scenes were being performed. I hoped to heaven that I could remember my lines. I also hoped, fervently, that Carter would discover something, or someone that would provide a key to unlock all the mysteries. He was putting up a good front tonight, yet I knew how tense he was underneath.

    I heard the sound of voices now in the hall, so I slipped behind the curtains and took my place behind the mock-up that was supposed to represent the front of Trollhaugen. It was really a set for a vampire's castle, but a few simple changes had made it apparent that it was supposed to be Trollhaugen.

    Ellie, with a long cape over her dress, trotted up and took her place alongside me. She grinned and squeezed my cold clammy hand.

    "Break a leg, kid," she said. "You'll be just fine, Molly. Don't worry."

    I could hear scrabbling sounds overhead and figured it must be Clive, getting into place on the roof.

    I heard the thud of footsteps on the stage followed by the sound of Carter's voice, telling the audience that this was to be a scene from a script which had never been performed. My heart was beating like a triphammer and it didn't slow down a bit when Carter announced the "debut" of a scintillating new performer.

The next thing I knew the curtains were parting and the audience was applauding politely.

"You're on, dear," Ellie hissed, and gave me a push.

I took a deep breath, swallowed and pushed open the door, speaking my first lines as I stepped onto the steps of a stage set that Carter had devised to resemble the steps in front of Trollhaugen. There were some murmurs of surprise when I was recognized.

Ellie stepped out after a moment and we played our little "saying goodbye" scene. The scene set the stage for what was to follow, and gave the information necessary for the rest of it to make sense. As Ellie walked away from me I realized that, despite my numb haze, I had said all my lines and that they must have been all right.

I raised my hand to wave after Ellie. Then I shivered and hugged myself, as if a cold breeze had suddenly come up.

I couldn't see a single face in the audience beyond the glare of the footlights. For all I knew, I was performing to an empty house. My knees felt shaky, but so far I was still remembering my lines. I stood for a moment more on the "steps", then turned to go into the house.

At that moment I heard a loud gasp from the

audience. It took no acting skill for me to jump to one side. I had almost forgotten the papier-mache stone Clive was to push off the roof. I jumped aside just in time for it to miss me.

Still in a state of numbness, I played out the rest of the scene. As far as I could tell, I didn't blow my lines or any bits of business.

In the second scene, I was to see Ellie, as the witch, in the Faraday garage. At the end of the scene I had to go off-stage, then come back on tattered and torn, the victim of a near-fatal automobile accident. I was still feeling numb in mind and body but I was gradually getting into the swing of it, my stage fright lessening. In the last part of the scene, I really hammed it up. I could only hope that someone in the audience was reacting to my endeavors and that Carter was watching them closely.

Finally, after what seemed like hours, the curtain closed for the last time to great applause. I took my bows feeling gauche and self-conscious, now that it was over.

Carter came loping up onto the stage to stand by my side. He gave me an encouraging smile. I leaned close to whisper, "Did anyone do anything suspicious...?"

The words lodged in my throat as I again heard gasps from the others, who had been moving out of their seats down below.

The footlights went out abruptly and someone said, "Oh, my God!" in a tense whisper.

Carter whirled around and stared at something behind me. I reacted more slowly. For a second, until my eyes adjusted to the change in light, I stared into the audience. I saw them, in turn, staring at something behind me on the stage.

I turned very slowly. The hair on my neck stood up, a phenomenon I had never before experienced.

There behind us, center stage, was the figure of a woman. A beautiful dark-haired woman hung by her neck from a heavy twist of rope. Nedra again. The figure was clear and the colors bright, yet you could see the red velvet curtains clearly through her body.

There was a heavy thudding sound behind me, but I couldn't make myself turn and look. I was hypnotized by the figure of Nedra swaying before my eyes.

I finally managed to tear my gaze away from the figure and look around for Carter. I was terribly afraid of what I would see in his face. His features were white and set, true, yet they didn't show the horror that had appeared there during the other incidents.

As suddenly as it must have appeared, the figure winked out. It was as though a light had been switched off.

Just at that instant I felt, rather than saw, Carter leap at me with a shout. He gave me a mighty shove that sent me sprawling, arms and legs flying wildly. I landed painfully on one hand and one knee, skidded across the rough floor for a few feet and ended up flat on my face.

On the edge of my consciousness I was aware of a whooshing sound, then a dull thwack followed by a third sound that made me think of a falling body. The stage shook from the impact.

Had something happened to Carter?

Chapter Eleven

Stunned, I finally mananged to turn over and gradually elevate myself into a sitting position. The palm of my hand and the knee that had struck the floor burned as if I had been holding them over a flame.

Remembering, I looked over to where Carter had been standing. He wasn't there. Instead, a huge sandbag swung gently back and forth like a pendulum, coming within a couple of feet of the stage floor.

In the seats immediately in front of the stage, Abner Snare and Emma were helping Carter to his feet. His face was contorted with pain. In the aisle he took a step, winced and almost fell.

I sat like a dummy where I was wondering what on earth had happened until Monica and Clive, who was out of his wolfman suit now, hurried over to help me to my feet.

"What happened?" I asked weakly.

"It all happened so fast," Monica said breathlessly. "A sandbag swung down out of the flies, that one you see there. It would have hit you, Molly, if Carter hadn't shoved you out of the way. You could have been killed!"

"It knocked Carter right off the stage," said Clive. "He's lucky if all he did was twist his ankle."

We got down off the stage. Carter and I were helped to chairs where we sat side by side. Ellie scurried off to find a First-Aid kit, while the rest of them clucked and worried around us.

Carter took my hand and gave it a squeeze. In spite of his pallor, he looked exhilarated; his eyes were bright and he looked more himself than he had for days.

Ellie returned with the First-Aid kit and began treating my skinned hand and knee. Clive examined Carter's leg and ankle. He said that they didn't seem to be broken, but that Carter should see a doctor as soon as possible.

Abner came back from examining the stage and the sandbag. His face wore a look of righteous indignation.

"That sandbag was rigged to be quickly released," he said. "I found this piece of rope and this section of wire lying on the floor backstage."

He held out his hand, showing us a short length of tightly woven rope and a piece of bent wire.

"Now who the hell did this?" he demanded, looking from one face to another.

Monica stared at him in apparent surprise. "Why, Abner, you can't possibly think it was one of us?" She looked around the group for confirmation. "We're all Carter's friends, and Molly's too, of course."

115

Abner glared at her. "Well, somebody did it and there's nobody here but us."

Monica looked confused. She glanced nervously around the group. "But who?" she whispered.

No one seemed to want to meet her eyes. I sneaked a look at Carter and caught him smiling slightly. I sensed that he was quite pleased Abner had taken it on his own to ask questions.

"All right, let's see what we can find out here," Abner said firmly. "Now, we know Molly and Ellie were on the stage. Clive, where were you?"

Abner, playing the questioning detective, was so completely different from his usual role that it would have been funny under different circumstances.

Clive was saying, "Why, I was backstage, getting out of my costume."

"You say you were in the dressing room, but I don't suppose there was anyone around to back you up on that? We'll just have to take your word?"

"No one." Clive shrugged. "So yes, you'll have to take my word for it."

"Was everyone else in their seats in the audience during the rest of the performance?" Abner looked at Carter. "You were watching, weren't you, Carter?"

Carter took his time about answering, looking thoughtful. He finally answered slowly, "I think most of them were but I couldn't watch everyone every minute. The only one I know for sure about is Raul. He got up near the end of the performance but he was only gone for a few minutes."

"Yes," Raul said calmly. "I simply had to go to the John. When I came back, I stood over there," he gestured toward the wall near the stage, "so that I wouldn't be blocking the view of the others. I couldn't have been gone for more than five minutes at the most. I'm sure of that."

"That's right," Emma said. "He was sitting right next to me for most of the time."

Abner confronted Clive. "Then that leaves you as the only one not accounted for."

Clive's face flushed a dark red. "Now listen! I'm not very happy about being placed on the spot like this. First of all she," he pointed to me, "asked me if I was here on Tuesday of last week. Then I figured out that someone wearing my wolfman costume tried to hurt her that day. And now, you're implying that I had something to do with all this!"

"Now, Clive." Abner held up his hand placatingly. "Nobody is really accusing you of anything. It was just a statement of fact. You *are* the only one who wasn't in plain sight when the sandbag swung down."

"Well, I can't help that, now can I?" Clive snapped.

"No," Carter said into the sudden lull in the conversation. "Don't worry, Clive. I'm sure no one really suspects you of having anything to do with what just happened but, as Abner pointed out, *somebody* did it. I'm naturally curious as to who, and why." He looked slowly around at his friends. "Now, I take it that you all saw what I saw just before I got sandbagged?"

"You mean Nedra?" Monica's voice was small. She shivered and rubbed her arms with her hands.

One by one, each of them nodded or mumbled an affirmation.

Carter said harshly, "Anybody have any ideas about what it was, or how it was managed?"

"It was Nedra," Monica said suddenly, still in that same small child-like voice. "It was her spirit, her ghost. She's come back to haunt us!"

The others looked at her with varying degrees of skepticism. Somebody laughed.

Monica flushed. "Well, it's possible," she said defiantly. "I mean, the magazines and Sunday supplements are full of articles about such things. Even science is taking them seriously today."

"Hogwash! Pure hogwash!" Emma snorted. "I may not know what it was but I do know that it was no ghost!"

Ellie shrugged her thin shoulders. "I'm not so sure, Emma. I think Monica's explanation is just as valid as any. In fact, so far, she's the only one to come up with any kind of explanation. Maybe it *was* Nedra's ghost, and maybe that's what caused the sandbag to break loose."

Abner held out the rope and the wire. "The bag had been previously rigged, remember. I don't think a ghost would find it necessary to do that."

"Well, it's not going to do us any good to chew over it all night." Roger St. James wiped his face with his handkerchief and gave me a tentative smile. "I, for one, am prepared to go home to bed. This has thoroughly unnerved me."

Clive, his normal disposition now somewhat restored, crossed his arms over his chest and announced firmly, "For my part, I think that we should search the house from top to bottom before we leave. We could spread out, each take different rooms. It wouldn't take us long."

Abner's smile was grim. "That's a great idea, Clive. And if one of us is the guilty party?"

Clive turned red in the face and fell silent.

"Say, what about that Alexander fellow?" Roger asked. "Where was *he* when it all happened?"

"That's a fair question," Abner said. "Why doesn't somebody go and fetch him?"

"I'll go," Clive said and left the room.

An uneasy silence fell during his absence.

Raul finally broke it. "You know, I would put it down to an over-active imagination, if only one of us had seen it, but when *all* of us saw Nedra up there... I don't know what to think."

"It was such a shock," Ellie whispered.

Belatedly, I realized that the thudding sound I'd heard behind me on the stage must have been Ellie fainting.

"You always were scared to death of Nedra, even when she was alive," Emma snapped, her voice cold and cutting. "So I'm not at all surprised you're afraid of her dead."

Ellie's cheeks pinked. "That's a mean thing to say, Emma." Weak tears appeared in the corners of her eyes.

Just then Clive returned with Alexander in tow and the discussion was cut short. Still, I was intrigued by the vibrations I felt during the brief exchange. I had a growing hunch that everyone in the room had their own secrets about Nedra. It gave me a creepy feeling.

Alexander, according to his story, had been in the kitchen with the catering people getting things cleaned up. He gave Carter a quizzical glance but did not ask what it was all about.

Carter raised himself, using only his hands on the arms of the chair, and tested his ankle by putting some weight on it. He grimaced with pain.

"Abner, I would appreciate it if you and Alexander would help me to my room. I think I'll make this ankle worse if I try to do it on my own."

Both Alexander and Abner stepped forward and helped Carter up, then supported him on either side as he turned to face us.

"My good friends," he said. "If you will excuse us, my wife and I are going to retire. This has been a trying evening to say the least."

Carter motioned for me to accompany him and we started out of the Chapel. The others were scurrying about, gathering up their belongings.

When we reached our room Carter thanked Abner, waited until he was gone, and told

Alexander to see everyone out. "Make sure they're *all* gone, then lock up tight."

Finally we were alone. I felt terribly tired, as if there had been a field of tension around us all evening which had now suddenly relaxed. Carter leaned back against the headboard.

He gazed at me and sighed heavily. "Well," he said, "Well, well, well!"

I sat down beside him and leaned my head on his shoulder. "You think you may have learned something?"

He put his arm around me tightly. "One thing I learned for sure tonight is just how precious you are to me, Molly. When I saw that sandbag coming at you, I was really terrified. If you had been killed...it would have been partly my fault, since I schemed this whole thing up!"

"Carter, don't think like that!" I scolded. Then I said softly, "You probably saved my life, darling. The whole thing is very frightening, isn't it?"

He smoothed back my hair and pulled my face down onto his chest. "Yes, it's frightening. Damned frightening. But at least now I feel we're on the right track. Whoever is doing this has to be a member of the club. One of my *friends*! There's no longer any doubt about that!"

I snuggled against him and, as I spoke, I could see the chest hairs stir with the expulsion of my breath. "I hate to mention this, but have you noticed that all the direct attacks have been against *me*? I mean, you've *seen* things but all the physical violence has been directed at me."

"I've noticed," he said grimly. "But you see, that could still be construed as an attack against me. You're the person I hold most dear in the world. If he, or she, destroys you, they destroy me, too, in the most horrible manner. That way, they figure I'll still be alive to suffer."

"That could be true, but there's something else...this has been the...what? Fourth attempt? All have failed. Our troublemaker is awfully incompetent. Else, he doesn't want to kill, just frighten."

His arms tightened around me. "Perhaps you've just been lucky, Molly. The brakes going out on your car, for example. That time you were damned lucky you weren't killed."

"I know, I remember." I shivered, then raised my face to his. "Anyway, I'm glad to know how important I am to you and I'd just as soon stay alive so that I can enjoy it."

"You will, darling. You will."

In the morning, Carter's ankle was swollen to twice its normal size and was a dull angry red. Alexander and I helped him into the Mercedes and Alexander drove us to the doctor's office. The doctor's examination disclosed pulled ligaments. He told Carter he would have to stay off his feet for at least a few days.

"I've been thinking," Carter said when we were back at Trollhaugen. "I'm not going to be able to get around much for several days but there are a couple of things I wanted to look into. Most of them will have to wait until I'm on my feet again, however, there's one thing I can do now."

"What's that?"

"Set up a watch in Nedra's room."

Since this had also occurred to me, the suggestion came as no big surprise.

"I'll have Alexander help me into the room at night. I'm not a heavy sleeper and we'll rig something, some kind of an alarm system."

"But won't it bother you?" I said slowly. "I mean, all those things reminding you of Nedra?"

Carter shrugged. "I'll just have to handle it." Seeing the look on my face, he added, "Don't worry, Molly. I'll be fine. I think I'm finally over that trauma, or whatever you want to call it."

He smiled brightly and he certainly, despite the ankle, looked fit and in control of himself. So why did I have this funny little gnawing feeling in the pit of my stomach?

"Well, if you're all that determined," I said. "What can I do to help?"

"You can just keep that pretty little head of yours out of any more danger!"

I looked at him, I knew, with sparks in my eyes. "Mr. Faraday," I said strongly, "you are looking at a liberated woman. I thought you knew that."

He had the grace to look chagrined. "I guess I did sound like a stereotype male chauvinist. But damn it, Molly, *anyone* is vulnerable when somebody is trying to kill them. I don't want you out running around, putting yourself in danger, making it easy for this person to get at you!"

"There's another thing I've noticed," I said thoughtfully. "All the attacks have been here, at Trollhaugen."

"That's true. But that may be because that's where you've been spending most of your time. Anyway, I think you're safer here. Maybe I should get someone to stay with you, someone to stay with you at all times. I've been thinking about that and I believe it's the best thing."

I thought of giving him an argument. The idea of some man hanging around watching me didn't appeal to me at all. But I thought I'd better not mention that. Instead, I said, "You still don't want to go to the police?"

He shook his head. "What I said before still applies. The publicity and the notoriety would be something fierce. Besides, there really isn't much the police can do, not until something actually happens."

"Yes," I said dryly. "Something like one of us getting killed."

"That won't happen, Molly. I won't let it. I promise." He spoke the words firmly and strangely. I believed him, at least in that moment.

"All right," I said. "So, who is going to be this boon companion of mine? I can't ask Aunt Bunnie. She has a full-time job and she lives clear across the country. Certainly not one of the club members! Not until we know who's doing this."

"A professional," Carter said calmly. "A

private detective, maybe. Maybe a woman. At least someone who has had that sort of training, someone who can be of some help in an emergency."

For a moment his suggesting a woman surprised me, then I leaned over and gave him a big kiss. "And I accused you of being a male chauvinist!"

He grinned. "I can't take credit where it's not due. Actually, I just don't want another man around you all the time. You're so lovely he might become distracted and not attend to his duties."

"Flatterer!" I kissed him again, enormously pleased. For a little while we forgot all about the things that threatened us.

Chapter Twelve

The bug was running beautifully after its repair job and check-up. As soon as I made sure that everything was working, I relaxed and tried to enjoy the trip down the hill into town. I just hoped that the radio station wouldn't pick this particular time to play "Pavanne for a Dead Princess". I didn't know if I was quite up to that.

Carter had spent the night in Nedra's room, with a thermos of coffee and a book. He had taken his pistol. He was an excellent shot and had a license for the gun but I had still worried about him. My worries had been needless since absolutely nothing happened.

Following his instructions, I had locked my bedroom door and promised not to open it for anyone but him. It had been an easy promise to keep.

I thought I would have no trouble falling asleep, since I felt a bone-deep fatigue. But as soon as I was in bed, I was wide awake, my head full of questions that had no answers. I did manage one decision before I finally drifted off sometime after midnight.

I very much wanted to talk to some of the individual members of the Club Macabre. I wanted to know what each of them knew about Nedra, what they thought of her. I have found that people will tell you a lot of things, if you have a sympathetic manner and if they are alone with you. I soon would have a "companion", so today would probably be my last chance to talk to the club members alone.

I lied to Carter. I told him that I was going shopping in Hollywood. I didn't actually *tell* him, I left him a note. He had been awake most of the night and was peacefully asleep in our bed when I left. He would probably be furious when he woke up and found me gone, but it was for a good cause.

I had called Ellie Stoval first, mainly because the exchange between she and Emma had intrigued me. Besides, Ellie was a quiet diffident little woman. I figured she would be easier to start with than some of the others, who were all pretty high-voltage personalities.

Ellie's small quaint stone-walled cottage was tucked into a corner of Laurel Canyon. An old-fashioned garden ran riot in the front. In the back I could see fruit trees and a square of green well-tended lawn.

Ellie answered the door wearing a long caftan. Her hair was pulled back in a braid and it seemed to me that her thin face looked tired. Without make-up, her eyes were washed out and pale.

She smiled gently when she saw me and escorted me into a comfortable room with a lived-in look, full of books and magazines. I accepted a cup of tea. After we were comfortably settled we sat and gazed at one another with the "Well, what now?" look of people who don't know each other very well.

I finally decided using disarming frankness would be best. I leaned toward her, smiled openly and said, "Ellie, I know you must be wondering why I wanted to see you."

She didn't deny it, just stared back at me expectantly.

"I want to know about Nedra," I said.

Her blue eyes seemed to film over and, for a moment, I feared that she had left me.

"You saw what happened the other night," I pressed on. "Well, other things have happened, too. The things in the scenes we did? They're all things that have happened to me."

She still looked vague and withdrawn. Obviously I wasn't getting through to her. I leaned closer and put all the sincerity I could muster into my voice. "Ellie, listen to me, it's important! I could have been killed by that sandbag, or any of the other times. When my car brakes failed, there was someone in the garage who looked just like you, someone dressed in your witch's outfit. Now, I'm not saying it *was* you, but I think you'll have to agree that it looks suspicious. Of course, if you don't want to talk about it, I can't very well force you to." I paused and settled back in my chair. "We could just go to the police."

That finally got a definite reaction. Her small mouth thinned and she looked at me, really looked at me.

"No!" she said quite loudly. "No, you mustn't

do that. They would stir it all up again...the newspapers...the gossip columnists...No! I'll tell you what I can, if you think it's important."

"I think it's important, Ellie. I think it's very important," I said quietly. "I'm sure the whole thing centers around Nedra somehow. Anything you can tell me might be of help. Emma hinted that you had been afraid of Nedra. Is that true?"

For a moment Ellie's faded eyes flashed and I had a glimpse of what she must have looked like when she was young; before time and life had chipped away at her.

"I wasn't *afraid* of her," she said with spirit. "It's just that she was a stronger personality than I. Some people are born leaders. Well, I guess I'm not one of them. But she was a strange woman, Nedra."

She said the name lingeringly and her eyes filmed over again, but this time with old memories. I tried to relax and let her talk.

"I met Nedra when I first came to Hollywood. We shared a room at the Eddington, a woman's boarding house on Vine Street. It's been torn down long since.

"Of course we had all come to Hollywood for the same purpose; we were all going to become famous movie stars. The movies were in their heyday then. Young people came from all over the country, like eager moths drawn into Hollywood's flame." She shook her head in a melancholy way.

"We were *so* young, so terribly young and full of hope. I had been studying dancing since I was six years old. I was going to be another

Eleanor Powell. Emma considered herself a serious actress. She had already been in a couple of plays on Broadway, and she came out here determined to compete with the Barrymores. And Nedra; well, Nedra was the mystery woman, even then. She never talked about her past the way the other girls did. I think most of the girls were always a little in awe of her. She wasn't the most beautiful girl staying at the Eddington, she didn't even have the best figure, but she had something else. She had that indefinable quality that we call, for lack of something better, 'star quality'. And she had a way about her that went even beyond that. People were drawn to her, especially men. She was young, of course. How young I never really knew. She was as quiet about her age as she was about everything else. But she instinctively seemed to know how to handle men, how to keep them flocking around. She was one of those women born with that knowledge.

"We all served our apprenticeship. We got up at dawn to answer 'cattle calls' for extras. We jostled and fought for bit parts, but Nedra was the only one who really made it big. She became, shall we say, acquainted with the head of one of the studios. After that, she appeared in a number of big-budget pictures. Many of them were 'sarong epics', which were popular then. She didn't have to do much more than look seductive and exotic on some South Sea island.

"Our paths separated about then. I began to get a few bigger parts and finally landed a good role in 'Help Me!'. It was a mystery picture, with overtones of horror. From there it was only a step to the real horror films, where I found my niche." Ellie smiled wryly.

"Unfortunately, I never did get to dance on the screen."

"And Emma?" I prompted.

"Emma drifted into horror films by another route. She was, and is, an excellent actress. But unfortunately, in Hollywood in those days, that wasn't enough. Let's face it, she had the face of a character actress. If she had come along today, when physical beauty doesn't matter so much, it might have been different for her. But in those days...

"Well, how many roles are there for a young character actress? The only place, it seemed, where there was steady work for her was in horror films.

"Nedra came back to us last of all. When the movies changed, when a compelling face and body weren't quite enough any more and they had stopped making jungle epics and harem films, even Nedra did not look quite so young and fresh as she once had. So she found a place along with us. We resumed our old friendship where we had left off. We were all manless at the time. I had been through two very unhappy marriages and had sworn to never try it again. Emma had never been married. Even Nedra, strangely enough, was temporarily between affairs, and/or husbands.

"Emma and I had been sharing a little bungalow near Metronome Studios and Nedra moved in with us. It was just like old times at first. Then Nedra met Carter Faraday." Ellie's voice stopped abruptly and I looked at her quickly, but her face was without expression.

After a moment she went on, "We were all working on the same film, 'The Pseudo Man'. Don't misunderstand, Molly. We all liked Carter. I mean, who could help liking him? He was handsome, friendly and outgoing. Nedra immediately went to work on him. It was easy to see that he was soon totally smitten."

Ellie began fumbling nervously with her hands, and I leaned forward encouragingly.

"This... well, this caused some bad feeling between Nedra and Emma. You see..." Ellie raised her face and looked directly at me.

"Emma had grown very fond of Nedra, very attached. She wanted to keep things like they were; the three of us together again. She didn't want a... she didn't want someone else intruding. She became very jealous and unreasonable and accused Nedra of making a play for Carter just to cause trouble.

"But Nedra told her that she really loved Carter and I believe she did. I still believe that. Carter was strong enough to handle Nedra. He wouldn't let her walk all over him and she liked that. In a short time they were married and she moved out of our bungalow. I don't think Emma every really forgave her, although she claimed that she did, and we were all still friendly afterward. Emma has what I guess you might call an implacable streak.

"When Nedra died I was afraid Emma might break down but you know, it was strange, she never shed a tear."

Ellie looked at me for corroboration of the

strangeness of this reaction, and I nodded my agreement.

"And that's all I know about Nedra. I don't know what this current business is all about." She looked down at the floor. "I can't think of anyone in our group who would want to hurt Carter. Or you, Molly. We all like you very much, you know. We all think you're good for him." She looked up at me and I saw sincerity in her pale eyes.

"I just wish that it would all stop. I'm getting too old for this kind of thing. Too old and too tired, I guess. I hope that what I've told you will be of some help."

I stood up, my mind full of the images of "old" Hollywood.

"Yes," I said thoughtfully. "It's too soon to tell for sure but I think it will help. It's certainly been very interesting. Thank you, Ellie."

As I walked out the door and down the path past the riot of flowers, I kept thinking of Emma Boles and Nedra.

Raul's house was quite different from Ellie's, and was very different from what I had been expecting. High in the Hollywood Hills, severe cubistic and plain, it presented a sheer blank wall to the road and anyone passing by, belligerently protecting its owner's privacy.

Raul had been very cordial on the phone when I told him that I wished to see him. I'm afraid I lied to him as well—I felt quilty about the fact that I was getting pretty good at lying—and told him that Carter had sent me because he was laid up with the ankle injury. It just seemed a good ruse to let him think it was someone else's idea.

After much time spent searching I finally found the entrance to the house, hidden in an inset doorway around to one side. It was a massive door, perfectly plain except for the symbol of an ankh carved into the wood. I knocked loudly, then noticed the bell rope and gave it a hard pull.

Raul answered the door himself. The interior of the house had an Oriental motif. There were some wonderful old pieces: a chest with dozens of drawers and an inlaid table. I would have liked to examine them more closely but, anxious to get my information and leave, I controlled my curiosity.

Raul offered me a drink, and to be sociable, I accepted. Raul looked very handsome, as usual. He was wearing a red velvet smoking jacket over a white shirt, the perfect picture of the urbane gentleman at home. He was smiling and friendly, perfectly at ease. I was beginning to think that nothing ever perturbed him very much.

As soon as we were settled with our drinks, served by an elderly Chinese houseboy, Raul said, "Now... what seems to be the problem, Molly?"

I placed my glass gingerly on the beautiful coaster on the end table beside me, arranged my thoughts, and said, "You saw what happened the other night?"

He nodded. "Yes, if Carter hadn't been hurt, I would have thought it all somebody's idea of a bloody joke. It's hard to imagine the sort of person who would do that sort of thing with serious intent."

I felt my temper starting to rise. This was not the first time that these near-fatal incidents had been dismissed lightly as a prank, or a joke. "Well, it certainly wasn't a joke! That was the fourth time my life has been threatened since I came to Trollhaugen. And there have been other strange unexplained things. Shadows on the wall, the harp in the music room playing 'Pavane for a Dead Princess' all by itself. Fun things like that." For some reason I didn't mention the shrine to Nedra in her room. Perhaps I was afraid Raul might think Carter was responsible for that.

Raul nodded again, thoughtfully, and took a sip of his drink. "Yes, Molly, I fully realize that these things aren't pranks. How has Carter been taking it?" His look was probing.

I averted my gaze. Again I felt driven to lie. For some reason I felt that I couldn't come right out and admit that Carter had been badly upset. I said, "He was startled, of course, and depressed but he's handling it quite well, I think."

"Good, I'm glad to hear it."

Was his smile faintly mocking? Or was it my over-active imagination?

I decided that it was time to get down to what I had come here for. "Raul, the reason I wanted to talk to you was because I would like you to give me any information you might have about Nedra. It seems clear that this whole thing revolves around her in some strange way.

Perhaps there's something in her past that might help explain it, give us a clue to what's going on."

He looked surprised, a little amused. "Nedra's past is pretty colorful, I grant you, but I can't think of anything that might be responsible for what you've told me has been happening."

Just tell me what you know, if you don't mind that is."

"Good Lord, no, my dear, I don't mind. Why should I mind?" He crossed his legs and cradled his glass in his palms. "I met Nedra Neal when I first came to Hollywood. I was a real Easterner. In fact, I had spent a great deal of time in England and California seemed pretty strange and exotic to me.

"I had been strictly a stage actor prior to coming out here. However, a Hollywood producer saw me in a play in New York, thought I was perfect for a picture he was doing and made me an offer I couldn't refuse. To make a long story short I found myself, in very short order, in fabulous Tinsel Town.

"I went right to work in the picture. On the set that first day I met Nedra, who was to be my co-star.

"She was already well-known by then. She was the darling of the head of the studio and she went from one Technicolor epic to another. They were making a lot of those bloody awful 'Island Princess' things and she seemed to star in all of them.

"This particular picture though was something a little different, more of a 'Harem

Princess', and it really wasn't too bad considering. Of course, at the time I was awfully conscious of being a 'legitimate actor', and went about saying things like 'all *real* acting is done on the stage, don't you know.' I must have been insufferable." Raul grinned, and shook the ice in his glass.

"Molly, let me freshen your drink." He rose, took my glass and walked over to the portable bar. As always, he was very graceful in motion. I had to admit that he was indeed a handsome man.

He brought me a drink and sat down again in his chair. "Now, where was I...? Yes. Well, Nedra was quite beautiful and I was very young and impressionable. She was very glamorous. To me she represented what Hollywood was supposed to be.

"We drifted into a rather short passionate love affair. Short because Nedra never stayed with one man very long. With her, it was always off with the old, on with the new. That sort of thing. That is, until she met Carter." He fell silent, a brooding look on his face.

After a moment he aroused and continued. "I was quite hurt at first, but then I began to see that it wasn't anything personal with Nedra. That was just her modus operandi, so to speak.

"After I came to see this we became friends, or at least as friendly as one could get with Nedra. Her temperamental vagaries made it difficult to sustain a relationship for very long.

"Through Nedra, I met Emma and Ellie. They had all known one another for several years; ever since they had come out to Hollywood to 'make it'. I had the feeling that their friendship hadn't worn too well with the years. Nedra had done so well and the other two, it seemed to me at any rate, were jealous.

"Emma, I gathered, had a thing for Nedra, which complicated matters. I shouldn't be at all surprised if she and Nedra were closer than close there for awhile...oh, don't look so surprised, Molly! Surely you're not shocked by anything movie stars do in their private lives?"

Feeling a touch embarrassed, I tried to shrug away my discomfiture. "I suppose I shouldn't be, but it's different when you're talking about someone that I know."

Raul laughed; a short bark of sound that seemed to have no relation to pleasure or amusement. "Don't worry. Emma's harmless. The years have mellowed her."

"I'm not worried," I said testily. "And I don't give a darn about her private life. She's a marvelous character and seems to be a very nice person. That's what counts."

He shrugged and gazed down into his glass. "A character, yes. I'll grant you that. A nice person? Well, I don't know."

I sat up alertly at the tone of his voice. "But I thought you two were good friends!"

He smiled wryly. "Molly love, in Hollywood, we all *seem* to be good friends; it's all a part of the 'Sweetheart, Baby Doll' syndrome. Oh, we get along fine but I don't think Emma's ever truly forgiven me for being Nedra's lover, however briefly.

"Anyway, to continue with my thrilling tale, one by one, for different reasons, each of us drifted into what is commonly called 'horror flicks'. And there, of course, we met Carter Faraday, who was already well established in the genre. I suppose you could say he was the Robert Redford of spooky movies.

"We all liked Carter immediately; he was, and is, a marvelously talented and charming man, as I'm sure you are aware by this time. But he created considerable upheaval among the ladies by capturing Nedra's affections. For once I believe Nedra truly cared for someone, or maybe it was just because she couldn't dominate Carter so easily. At any rate, theirs became a much publicized and glamorized romance, finally culminating in matrimony.

"Strangely enough, it was Ellie who seemed more upset by the marriage than Emma. I think perhaps Ellie had a crush on Carter. She had played a number of roles in his films and I believe Carter paid some attention to her, just being nice I would imagine, before Nedra came into his life.

"And that's about all the background, Molly. After the marriage things settled down and smoothed over. We all stayed friendly and developed our own little coterie, so to speak. We worked together in many films. Nothing of any importance happened to any of us until Nedra died so tragically."

He set his glass down on the coffee table. "So that's about it, love. The story of Nedra Neal in Hollywood, as I knew it. Are you any wiser now than before you heard it?"

"Maybe," I said, and smiled thoughtfully. "Tell me something, Raul. Did the police ever consider Nedra's death anything other than an accident?"

Raul gave me a sharp look, then lowered his gaze to the cigarette he was lighting. "They considered all angles, I am confident, but the final and official verdict was that it was an accident."

"What do you think?"

He glanced up and exhaled smoke before answering. "I accepted the police explanation, Molly. Oh, I don't doubt that there were many people who would have been blissfully happy to do Nedra in, including the director of that last picture, but there was not the slightest evidence ever found to show that it was anything *but* an accident."

I stood up. "Well, thanks for your time, Raul. I do appreciate your talking to me. I'd better get home now, before Carter starts to worry about me."

Raul stood also and, gently taking my elbow, walked with me out to the street.

"Carter loves you very much, you are very precious to him. He wants to protect you from any unpleasantness, I am sure of that, Molly."

His touch on my arm was making me nervous and, as I too often do, I found myself attempting to control the nervousness with chatter. "Yes, Carter is protective. He's very concerned about me. For instance, he's hiring a female bodyguard to stay with me at all times. At least he's looking for one." I laughed lightly. "I only hope she doesn't look too much like a lady wrestler."

We stopped near my little car. Raul looked

deep into my eyes and said seriously, "I don't blame him for hiring a woman. If I had a wife as lovely as you, Molly, I wouldn't trust a male bodyguard with her, either."

I forced a smile and gave him the required peck on the cheek. His words had been flattering, so why did they unsettle me? I hurriedly got into the bug and started the engine. As I drove away I could see him, in the rear view mirror, still standing at the curb before his house, staring after me.

Chapter Thirteen

Ms. Sandra Hooper looked like a stereotype librarian, very subdued and sensible looking. She wore her hair in a bun and looked to be in her late thirties.

She wore a neat well-tailored blue suit and medium-heeled shoes. Behind the huge mod glasses her eyes were large and blue. Her expression was reserved and lady-like. In fact, I guess that's what impressed me the most. I hadn't expected a woman bodyguard to look so lady-like.

I smiled and stuck out my hand. "Hi, I'm Molly Faraday."

She gave me a small reserved smile in return and took my hand. "I'm Sandra Hooper." Her handshake was firm, no-nonsense.

"Alexander will show you to your room," said Carter, motioning to Alexander to pick up her suitcase. "We've put you in the room next to Molly's. There's a connecting door."

She nodded gravely. "Good."

"We'll be in the small parlor. When you come down, you can join us in a drink."

She nodded and smiled again, then turned

and followed Alexander up the stairs. We watched as she walked away from us, looking trim and efficient. Her legs weren't too good, yet she walked gracefully and held her head high.

"Well, what do you think?" Carter asked, after she was out of hearing.

I said hesitantly, "I'm not sure yet. She looks capable enough, but not very tough."

He laughed and squeezed my waist. "What did you expect her to look like, a lady athlete?"

"I suppose I did, in a way. Where did you find her?"

"I asked Alf to contact all the agencies and ask each to send around their best operative. From what Alf said when I talked to him about it, there aren't all that many. I guess it's a field that doesn't attract too many women. *Ms*. Hooper," he accented the title, "was evidently the best qualified. At least she must have impressed Alf, since she's the only one to show up so far. She has good references and she seems to know her business. Since we do need someone right away, I hired her on the spot. I called Alf to tell him not to send anyone else around, but he's out of town. I left word with his secretary."

Carter lowered his head until he was staring directly into my eyes. "Now, Mrs. Faraday, I want you to listen to me carefully. You are to keep this woman with you at all times. No more of this running off by yourself, as you did the other day. I'm going to be paying her a good deal of money to see that you don't get hurt, so I hope you won't make it difficult for her by sneaking off on your own. I want your promise!"

I experienced a mixture of guilt, annoyance and love. Guilt for having lied to him and sneaked off to talk to Ellie and Raul, annoyance that he was treating me like a child, and love because he cared enough to want to protect me from harm.

"I am not a child, Carter," I said with dignity. "However, I will do as you ask. I know you're asking it for my own good. Also, I have no really great desire to be killed by a falling stone, runaway car, sandbag, or whatever. I shall cleave unto Ms. Hooper as I would a sister. I shall not leave her side, except to go to the biffy!"

Suppressing a grin, he looked at me with a mock scowl. "You sound suspiciously meek to me but I suppose I'll have to take your word. Now, let's go have a cocktail while we wait for Ms. Hooper to come down."

He limped off toward the small parlor and I followed. We were about halfway through our drinks—Sandra Hooper had not yet joined us—when the phone rang in the study next door.

Alexander answered it. In a moment he came into the room where we were, carrying the phone. There was a peculiar look on his face.

Carter said, "Who is it, Alexander?"

Alexander's handsome face registered bewilderment. "They won't say. They want to talk to you. The voice sounds...well, strange, like it's disguised or something."

I put down my drink and watched as

Alexander plugged the phone into the wall outlet. He then placed the instrument on the table next to Carter.

Carter gave me a glance, in which I read apprehension, before picking up the receiver.

"Hello," he said. "Yes, this is Carter Faraday."

There followed an interminable silence, as Carter listened without saying another word. I watched the play of expression on his face.

Finally, face like a thundercloud, he shouted, "No way!" He slammed down the receiver.

"Who was it?" I demanded.

He shook his head. There was an angry, baffled look on his face. "They wouldn't say. I couldn't even tell if it was a man or a woman. They said that, if I wanted to find out who is causing the 'disturbances' here at Trollhaugen, I must go down to the old Metronome Studios tonight at eight."

"You can't do that, Carter. You can't even walk!"

"I told him that. He, or she, said if that were the case, I should send you. I told him..."

"I heard what you told him. What about Sandra Hooper?"

He stared. "What about her?"

"Why can't I go, if she goes along with me?"

He shook his head firmly. "No, Molly. Absolutely not! It's far too dangerous. Someone has already tried to kill you several times. Going to an old abandoned studio at night would be foolhardy. I refuse to let you risk it!"

"But if Ms. Hooper..."

"If Ms. Hooper what?"

We both turned at the sound of Sandra Hooper's voice. She was just coming into the room.

"We just got a strange phone call," I said excitedly. "A mysterious stranger wants Carter to meet him, or her, at the old Metronome Studio this evening. The person on the telephone said they have information about the things that have been happening to us."

Sandra looked at Carter. "Of course you can't go because of your ankle."

Carter nodded. "That's right. Then the caller said to send Molly. Naturally I said, no way."

Sandra looked thoughtful. "Maybe you're making a mistake, Mr. Faraday."

Carter frowned in astonishment. "A mistake? You mean you think Molly should go? After all that has happened? I've told you how close she's come to being killed!"

"I mean I think *we* should go. I think I can assure you that I can protect Mrs. Faraday from harm. It's what you employed me to do."

"Two women alone?" he said incredulously.

Sandra's smile was wry. "That's a very chauvinistic remark, Mr. Faraday. I am a more than competent operative. It's what I was trained for and I do it well. You employed me to be a companion and bodyguard for your wife. Don't you now think I'm capable of doing the job?"

If I hadn't been so directly involved, I would have laughed aloud at the expression on Carter's face.

"Sandra's right, Carter," I said. "We should go. If there's any chance... Carter, we've got to get to the bottom of this thing. I don't believe we can afford to pass up *any* chance at getting information!"

"Well, you certainly haven't been passing up very many," he said grumpily. "But I don't feel right about this. I forbid you to go!"

"Carter, I *must*! I can't go on this way much longer. We have to settle this thing, get out from under it."

"No! And that's final."

Metronome Studios had been a thriving place once; full of life, glamor and excitement. Now, it was only a ghost of its former self. For awhile, I had been told, it had been used for television but now even that activity had ceased. The lot had been sold to land developers. The buildings squatted quietly, waiting for the bulldozers and the wrecking ball.

To me there was something infinitely sad about the abandoned studio. A dream factory with no more dreams to produce. It made me feel as if the world were running out of dreams; and perhaps it is.

Sandra drove as efficiently as she did everything else. During the drive out she briefed me on what to do and how to act, in case of an emergency. She seemed to know what she was talking about.

I was keyed up and nervous; high on a mixture of adrenalin and excitement.

Sandra parked the car neatly against the curb near the high iron gates of Metronome Studios—gates separating the real world from the make-believe. I soon found out just how efficient she was. With a slender piece of steel from her purse, she jimmied the big lock on the gates and we were inside.

After a few moments I decided that nothing was lonelier or spookier, than a deserted movie studio at night. The moon was bright. The spaces between the buildings were dappled with shadows that seemed to move in the brisk wind that pushed debris along the sidewalk, and shook the branches of the trees.

I shivered, and buttoned my jacket against the touch of chill that the wind carried.

Sandra seemed not to notice either the wind or the cold. Head up, she sniffed the air like a hunter. "Where did this caller say to meet him?"

I shivered again but not from the cold this time. "In Sound Stage Number Three. I hope they still have the electricity on in there."

"I hope so, too, but at least we have flashlights."

"Yes," I said, hefting the long heavy flashlight in my hand. Its weight gave me a little comfort, not much, but some. I was having misgivings about the wisdom of this little expedition. I had just about decided that this wasn't the most intelligent thing I had ever done, however, it was too late now.

"We might as well get on with it. It's nearly eight o'clock." Sandra started toward one of the long low buildings. I followed after.

"How do we find Sound Stage Three?" I asked.

"I was here once, shortly before it shut down.

As I remember, it's near the entrance, a very large building. If I'm not mistaken, it's this one here."

She pointed to the building we were approaching.

"I wonder why he wants to meet me here?" I said.

We were almost to the building. I could sense rather than see Sandra's shrug. "Who knows what goes on inside people's heads? He has to be some kind of a mental case to do this sort of thing anyway."

"Thanks," I said dryly. "That's really encouraging."

The white of Sandra's smile flashed in the moonlight. "Of course, it could be someone who just likes movies, or movie studios. Someone a little eccentric, you know?"

Well, I thought, that description could fit just about any of the members of the Club Macabre.

"I just hope you're as good a bodyguard as your recommendations say you are, Sandra."

Sandra tried the knob of the door. It opened smoothly inward, revealing an inner rectangle of unrelieved darkness. "Don't worry, Molly. I'll look after you."

She fumbled just inside the door, directing the beam of her flashlight against the wall. Suddenly the place was flooded with bright light. I had to clamp my eyelids shut against the glare.

"At least the lights are on. That should be a comfort to you." Sandra strode briskly into the huge building. I hesitantly followed in her wake, my heart beating fast.

The interior of the building was a bewildering jumble of sets, flats, arc lights, cranes, catwalks and miscellaneous equipment—the debris of forty years of film making washed up here by the waves of time. We stopped and, as the echoes of our footsteps died away, there was no other sound to be heard in the vast hanger-like building.

"Where do you suppose he is?" I whispered to Sandra.

"I don't know," she said matter-of-factly, in an ordinary speaking voice. "Perhaps you should call to him."

I stared at her. *"Call?"*

She shrugged. "Suit yourself."

"Hello," I called tentatively, then louder, "Hello, is anybody here? This is Molly Faraday!"

My voice echoed and bounced back to me, sounding like a bad recording, but there was no answer.

"Now what shall we do?" I turned to Sandra, who seemed blessedly cool and sure of herself.

She led the way, setting off at a brisk pace, and I followed again, feeling definitely apprehensive now. At any other time, I would have been enchanted by the chance to wander around among these artifacts of a business that had always fascinated me, but tonight they only served to add to my fear and confusion. We stepped over broken equipment and came to a dead end against set walls. There was still no sound other than that made by Sandra and I.

After retracing our steps and taking another

direction, we came abreast of an artificial tunnel, at least it looked like a tunnel. Sandra stopped short. "Sh-h," she said. "I think I heard something. You stay here, Molly."

She motioned me back and stepped inside the tunnel. Very quickly, she vanished from my sight. I had just time to wonder why she hadn't turned on her flashlight, as it was dark inside, when I heard her scream.

The sound cut through the dusty silence like a siren blast. For a moment I was stunned into immobility. I stood undecided. Then, without further thought, I plunged in after her. At least I remembered to flick on my flashlight.

I was only a few steps into the tunnel, when the lights went out in the big room behind me. My heart gave another lurch. My first thought was thankfulness that I had the flashlight, then panic struck as I looked down at the beam thrown by the flash. It was dim and wavery. Even to my un-mechanical eye it was apparent that it was soon going to go out and leave me in total darkness.

I stood quite still, trying to fight down a wave of hysteria, and collect myself. Just when I thought I had my fear under control, I discovered a new cause for panic. The floor beneath my feet was beginning to move. Slowly at first and then with increasing violence, the floor was undulating and shaking.

"My God!" I said aloud. "It's an earthquake!"

I had visions of myself being buried under sets and props as the roof of the building came down around me. I had heard tales of earth tremors, mild and severe, but this was my first experience and it was frightening.

I put my hand on the wall for support but it was shaking as much as the floor. A sudden more violent shake hurled me to my knees. The dimming flashlight jumped out of my hand, went bouncing away from me and winked out. I wasn't sure whether I should stay where I was, or try to get outside. For some reason I couldn't remember all the sensible things you are supposed to do during an earthquake. I only knew that instinct was telling me to get out of this tunnel.

I managed to get to my feet and, lurching and staggering, made my way toward the entrance, or at least toward where I *hoped* the entrance was. When I had gone a few feet, my toe hit something that clanked and rolled.

"The flashlight!" I thought hopefully, bending down for it. I nearly fell again but, thank God, it *was* the flashlight. Even if the batteries were good for only a few minutes, it was better than total darkness.

By this time I realized that the earthquake had been going on for quite a long while, much too long, and that there was a curious regularity to it. Then, all of a sudden, I stepped out of the tunnel. My right hand, which had been feeling along the wall, encountered nothing but air. In a moment I was standing on a floor blessedly still and solid beneath my feet. The earthquake had stopped.

I stood there for several seconds, panting, utterly baffled by the sudden cessation of violent movement. Then I realized that a grinding noise was still continuing behind me. I had to risk the use of the flashlight. I had to *know*. I turned and pointed the light at the source of the sound. The light was faint and did not reach far, but it was enough to show me what my "earthquake" had been. In that brief flash of watery light, I saw the floor and the walls of the tunnel buckling and rolling. The earthquake had been a local affair. It was a prop, a set, contrived to simulate a real earthquake. My relief was enormous.

However, it was short-lived. I was safe from the earthquake, but where in the world was Sandra? And who had turned on the switch that had activated the tunnel?"

First of all I had to find Sandra. Presumably she had a gun and knew how to use it. I recalled that she had promised to protect me. A fat lot of good that was going to do me, if I couldn't find her.

"Sandra?" I called tentatively, then louder, "Sandra!"

My voice rolled around the room and vanished somewhere above me. The tunnel was still grinding away but there was no other sound.

If Carter's caller wanted to harm me, I thought, the first thing he would do was get rid of my bodyguard.

That thought did nothing to cheer me. It seemed the only choice I had was to find my way out of this horrible place as quickly as possible. If something had happened to Sandra, if she had been waylaid by our mysterious caller, if she was now lying somewhere knocked out and tied up, I could do her more good by going for help than by blundering around this nightmarish place in total darkness.

I bravely started forward then stopped short. Where was the door? I hadn't the faintest idea in which direction to go. I risked another flash from the failing light to orient myself, then started off in the direction I seemed to remember we had come. I was making slow progress, using the light only when I came up against a seemingly impossible barrier directly across my path. I tried to keep my mind focused on what I was doing. If I let myself think about the darkness, or about the fact that I was all alone, panic began to nibble at the edges of my thoughts.

As I felt my way around the corner of a stage wall, I heard the sound. Surely there is no sound in the world more frightening than the sound of heavy breathing when you have no clue as to its source. I don't know why, but it's true; ask anyone who has had a "breather" call.

Now, behind me in the almost total darkness, I heard it again; so loud and rasping that it surely could not be a human breathing. No human could have lungs large enough to draw in that horrible rasp of air.

My neck felt cold as ice. Collecting all my courage, I whirled around, switching on the weak flashlight.

Chapter Fourteen

The fading flashlight flickered once, then winked out; but that one brief wash of light had outlined a nightmare figure that stayed in my mind's eye long after it was swallowed up by darkness.

A huge head lolled sideways on a squat neck, long arms swung near the floor, and a large misshapen hump weighed down its back. The creature had smiled at me—a grotesque grimace—showing broken yellowed teeth like fangs, and rubbery twisted lips.

As I was once more plunged into darkness, I realized that never before had I felt the force of such terror. I knew it was foolish of me to run blindly. I knew that I should remain as calm as possible; that I placed myself in far more danger by losing my head, but some primitive part of me shrieked "Run!", and I ran.

I crashed into set walls and tripped over boxes and light cables, scarcely feeling the pain. Suddenly, I was trapped. I could feel nothing but walls around me. I must have stumbled around the enclosure for some time before my mind grasped the fact that I could go no farther. With that realization came a degree of sanity. The building was like a huge maze and I must have run into a dead end. But I had gotten here by some entrance, and so there had to be a way out.

My heart was thudding painfully. The breath burned in my throat. I stood very still, listening for footsteps creeping up on me, but I heard nothing. Slowly I sank down onto the rough surface of what seemed to be a wooden crate. My legs and arms were beginning to hurt from the bruises and cuts I had collected during my mindless flight. I was exhausted by physical exertion and hopelessness. I felt that I could not go one step farther.

And Sandra. My God, what had happened to Sandra? Was she still alive? I felt sorrow thicken my throat and tears burned my eyes. What was I going to do?

Then I heard the breathing again. I jumped to my feet and whirled around, but it was impossible to pinpoint the direction it was coming from. It seemed to come from all around me. Then I heard the words; words so full of blind hate and murderous venom that my mind shrank away from them. The voice was sexless, flat and soft, as it repeated the dreadful litany. The name of Nedra appeared frequently in the droning recitation. Later, I couldn't recall many of the words, only their intent.

The owner of the disembodied voice wanted me dead, of that there was no doubt. I was to be a sacrifice in the name of Nedra, my death would expiate the sins that I had committed against her memory when I had married Carter. Also, my death would hurt Carter, that seemed to be an important part of the plan. I would never forget one phrase which was repeated several times: "He will be hurt as I was hurt! He will suffer as I have suffered!"

Then followed a mind-stunning list of the things the speaker was going to do to me; all recited in that horrible flat unaccented voice. I felt as if I were going mad and I knew that whoever the voice belonged to was insane.

I felt the panic edging back inside my mind. My body trembled with the effort to hold myself together. As the voice droned on, I tried to shut it out. I began feeling my way around the walls again; carefully inch by inch. Then my hand touched air and I experienced a surge of hope. I followed my groping hand, walking as silently as I could, trying not to bump into walls or trip over unseen hazards on the floor. Cautiously, step by step, I advanced. The voice was some distance behind me now, evidently assuming that I was still a captive, or maybe not caring; maybe so wound up in his, or her, own sick fantasy that it didn't matter if I was still there or not.

Painfully slow, I inched along. The voice was fading now as the distance between me and my tormentor widened. Then a horrendous banging sound almost startled me into a dead faint. I stopped, frozen against a wall, until I realized that someone on the outside was banging on the building, attempting to get in. Suddenly, over the pounding, I heard my name called.

"Molly! Molly, are you in there!"

It was Carter's voice. Nothing had ever sounded so good to me. I didn't dare answer since I didn't want to give my location away to whoever, or whatever, was in this place with me. However, now that I had a direction to focus on, I hurried toward the sounds going as fast as I dared.

The pounding and the shouting kept on. I prayed that it would continue until I could make my way to the door. I ran into another dead end and, in a frenzy of impatience, I felt around and around for what seemed like hours, until I found my way out again.

The pounding had now changed to heavy thuds. They must be trying to break down the door, I thought. Then, suddenly, I felt nothing against my groping hands and I knew that I was in the open. I found myself sobbing with relief, for the sounds made by my rescuers were very close now. In another moment, my hands touched the cold smoothness of a door knob. Then I was almost knocked flat as the door burst inward. Two shadowy forms charged toward me.

After the stygian darkness of the studio, the faint light from outside seemed amazingly bright. Then all the lights of the studio came on. I was blinded by the glare and almost smothered in someone's arms. In a flurry of confusing noise and movement, I was handed into another pair of arms and found blessed refuge against my husband's chest. No place had ever seemed so much like home to me. I didn't realize I was sobbing, until Carter tenderly wiped my face with his handkerchief and kissed my tears away.

"It's all right now, Molly darling," he said gently. "It's all over, you're safe."

They spent two hours, Alf and Alexander, searching for Sandra but did not find a trace of her. There was also no sign of my tormentor. For all the interior of the sound stage building showed, he might have existed only in the depths of my own mind.

I sat in the Mercedes with Carter, while Alf and Alexander searched the building. After a good stiff drink of brandy and some cuddling and comforting, I was in condition to listen to what had happened after Sandra and I left Trollhaugen.

After Sandra and I had left Carter alone in the small sitting room, Alf had called. During the conversation, Carter mentioned that he thought Alf had done well in selecting Sandra as my bodyguard. Alf had reacted with great surprise. Not only had he not interviewed Sandra, he had never heard of her. That was the reason for his call. He had been puzzled when his secretary had relayed the message to him that Carter had employed the first applicant sent over. He had sent no one!

Carter told me that this bit of information hit him like a karate chop. Who was this woman into whose care he had entrusted me?

He and Alexander had gone looking for us. Finding us gone, he knew immediately that we had sneaked off to the studio.

"And if you *ever* do anything like that again, I'll lock you in your room and throw away the key!" he said harshly. "You don't know the hell I've been going through this past hour!"

"I'm sorry, darling," I said humbly, truly contrite. "It was the stupidest thing I've ever done in my entire life."

"With that, I can agree!"

After Carter had found us gone, he called Alf back and asked him to meet them at Metronome Studios. When Carter arrived there with Alexander, they found my bug parked on the street, so they more or less knew we were still inside. The door to Sound Stage Number Three was locked and barred. They had had no choice but to break it down. Carter had been terribly upset; not knowing whether they would find me dead or alive.

"I don't understand, Carter," I said, when he was finished. "Who *is* Sandra?"

Carter shook his head and pulled me closer in the warm darkness of the back seat. "I have no idea. As far as the hunchback you saw, I'd say he's the same person who's been causing the trouble—our mysterious friend in disguise again. But I don't understand how Sandra's involved, although I am sure now that she set us up for this. She knew who made the call to me and helped to lure you out here. But I don't know why."

"But Sandra's not one of your group and you've been sure all along that it was someone you knew."

He shifted his arm to push a stray strand of hair out of my eyes. "It's possible that Sandra *is* someone from the group, Molly, and we just didn't recognize her."

"How could she be? You know all those people well. She really would have to be a master of disguise."

"Exactly." Carter was nodding. "After all, so far you've been attacked by a wolfman, a witch, a vampire, and now a hunchback, so somebody is pretty damned good at making physical changes."

I turned to snuggle closer into his arms, accidentally bumping his injured ankle with the toe of my shoe. He gave a smothered gasp. Guilt immediately swept over me.

"Darling, your poor foot! I forgot all about it. You were supposed to keep off it."

He laughed wryly. "Well, under the circumstances...."

At that moment Alf and Alexander, flushed and breathing heavily from their efforts, came hurrying up.

"Not a sign of anyone," Alf said. His face was pale and he had a smudge of dirt on one cheek. "We went through every inch of that building. Nobody's there. Of course, it's a big lot, many buildings. To search them all would take all night, anyway it's likely that whoever it was is long gone by now."

"Maybe we should call the police?" Alexander asked.

"And tell them what?" Alf responded. "No, if we call the police in, the whole thing is going to come out. Then it will get full media treatment.

Carter doesn't want that. Besides, I figure that Ms. Sandra Hooper can take care of herself. She lied her way into this and she can jolly well get herself out, *if* she's in any danger. Somehow, I don't believe she is."

"I agree," Carter said firmly. "In my opinion, she's as much involved in this as the person who was doing the hunchback number. For now, I'd better get Molly home and into bed."

"Sounds like a lovely idea," I said drowsily, with my face pushed against Carter's chest. Reaction was setting in now, and I felt that I could sleep the clock around.

I did more than sleep the clock around. I fell into bed some time after midnight and slept until almost dark the next afternoon.

When I did awake I couldn't understand, at first, why my body felt as if I'd been playing football, with me as the ball. I got out of bed and peered at myself in the mirror.

A pretty sight, my girl, I thought, looking at the pale bruised female staring back at me from the glass. I had a real lulu of a purple mark on one cheek. My legs and arms were a mass of bruises. I scowled at my mirrored image and turned away.

Despite the long sleep, or perhaps because of it, I felt sluggish.

The sound of the bedroom door opening drew my attention. Carter stuck his head inside, smiled broadly when he saw me up and limped on into the room.

"Well!" he said. "Sleeping beauty has finally arisen. About time, too."

I made a face denoting chagrin. "Not much of a beauty at the moment. Try me again in a few days, after my bruises have all healed."

He hobbled over to me, took me in his arms and kissed me soundly. "You're beautiful to me, Molly. Now, how about some dinner? Do you want to walk downstairs or would you rather have it up here?"

I thought for a moment. "In here, I think. We can build a fire, put the little table in front of the fireplace and pretend we're honeymooners."

He laughed and tickled my ribs, a trick that never failed to send me into fits of girlish laughter.

"Your wish is my command, O Princess," he said with great originality. Performing a salaam, a little clumsily because of his injured foot, he backed from the room.

I set a match to the logs which were already laid in the grate, pulled up the soft blue chair before the hearth as the flames caught and sat down with a sigh. I felt better already. There is nothing like the attentions of a man to perk a woman up. I knew that once I had some food in me I would feel better still. If it weren't for the terrifying series of events that had been making us both miserable, I thought, I would be the happiest and most contented woman in the world.

Thinking about those events was a mistake. The whole thing pushed its ugly way into the forefront of my mind again and wouldn't leave.

What were we going to do now? Carter seemed to think we were getting nearer to a solution. But it struck me that we were just as far away from clearing up the mystery as we had been in the beginning. We had learned some things, yes, but nothing that would really help us locate the person responsible.

When Carter returned a few minutes later, I was feeling depressed again. He sensed my mood as he came into the room. "Cheer up, Molly. Alexander is whipping up a great repast. He'll be up in a little while with it. What's wrong, darling? Been thinking about all this again?"

I nodded, sighing. "I'm afraid so. I can't seem to get it out of my mind. Carter, are you going to spend the night in Nedra's room again?"

He made a face. "I don't really think it would do any good. Our tormentor seems to know when I'm there, then doesn't put in an appearance. I think I might as well give it up."

For some reason, I had a strong reaction to this. Anger flared for a moment. I almost snapped back that he didn't seem to *want* to learn the truth, but I bit my lip hard and for once kept my mouth shut. Maybe he was right, so I just smiled. We had our candlelight supper in front of a toasty fire. For a little while, we both forgot about hanging women and strange monsters trying to kill me.

Yet, some time later, as Carter lay sound asleep in our bed, I sat wide awake in the chair before the dying fire. I still couldn't help but think that we should "stake out" Nedra's room.

Instinct and/or intuition made me think this. And logic told me that, where there was a shrine, there had to be a worshipper. I was sure that the answer we sought—at least a large part of it—lay in that room. I had done nothing but sleep for twelve hours, so I decided to spend some of the night watching.

I stood up. Nedra's room was probably still locked, but I had gotten in once before without a key.

Chapter Fifteen

It was chilly in Nedra's room. I looked longingly toward the canopied soft-looking bed, then trudged with my armful of blankets and pillows to the room's one closet.

I felt very uncomfortable; so much of Nedra was still in the room.

None of the candles were lit, yet there seemed to be...

I sniffed. I was certain there was a strong odor of burned wax in the room.

I couldn't resist a peek into the casket. The mannequin was lying there in simulated repose. I suppressed a shiver and hurried into the closet.

Within a very few minutes I had a cozy nest built on the floor of the large clothes closet. After turning off the room light, I settled down with my flashlight—filled with fresh batteries—a thermos of coffee and my watch, which had a luminous dial. I carefully fixed the door so that it was slightly open and settled back to wait.

As the time dragged past without incident, I found myself becoming increasingly nervous. I questioned the wisdom of my even being here. The closet was filled with the heavy scent of gardenia perfume. When I moved, even slightly, the hanging garments brushed my face and head. It felt, disturbingly, as if I were being touched by the ghostly fingers of Nedra, herself.

I found myself listening for even the slightest noise, listening so hard there was a faint singing sound in my ears. About one a.m. I could have sworn I heard sounds coming from the direction of Nedra's casket. But, when I flashed the light that way, nothing, either alive or dead, was there.

Even full of coffee and the best of intentions, I must have dozed. As I struggled back up through the cobwebs of sleep, I became conscious of a low droning humming sound. I saw light coming through the crack in the closet door. Terror struck at me before I was fully awake.

It took me a moment or two to sort things out, to remember where I was and what I was doing there. When I finally had it all put together, I leaned carefully forward, putting my eye to the partially open door.

Fear and excitement made me tremble. I almost bumped my head on the door frame, but then my eyes made the adjustment to the light, and I could see the figure in front of Nedra's casket.

The two candles on either side of the altar were now burning. The fitful red light from the glass candleholders splattered the walls like eerie patterns sketched in blood. In front of the casket was a large candelabra holding three candles. The figure, cowled and sexless, knelt in front of this candelabra, reciting some sort of droning litany.

I could feel the hairs on the back of my neck raise. A sick feeling began to spread through my stomach. The voice was the same one I had heard on the abandoned sound stage. I was sure of it! That meant here, no more than a few feet away, was the probable answer to our questions, the solution to our problem. But what was I going to do?

I realized that there was a large flaw in my plan for this evening. I had only thought things through to the point of discovering the identity of our mystery person. I hadn't really considered just what I was going to do when I found him, or her. If it was a woman, I supposed I would have at least an equal chance to overpower her, if she weren't carrying a weapon. But if it was a man, what chance would I have? After all, this was probably the same person who had tried to kill me several times already.

As I crouched there, mentally engaged in my problem, the figure rose slowly to its feet. It lifted the silver candelabra high overhead in a sort of gesture of... of what? Worship? Idolatry? Then the candelabra was lowered until the light was shining on the interior of the casket. Something about the way the figure moved its arms was familiar. Could it be Carter? Had he been lying to me, misleading me all along?

My heart told me that it wasn't possible, it simply couldn't be Carter. But, my head reminded me of all the incidents that had occurred. At that instant, I would have given anything to have known whether or not Carter was asleep in our bed in the room down the hall.

I thoughtfully hefted the solid weight of the flashlight gripped in my hand. If I switched it on from this distance, chances were that I wouldn't be able to see who it was. The large cowl collar effectively hooded the face. Also, that would certainly alarm whoever it was. Then it would run out of the room before I could get out of the closet. Of course, I could always sneak out of the closet in the darkness, creep up close behind and shine the light in its face.

The problem was, *then* what would I do? If it was Carter, I wouldn't care. If it was Carter, I wouldn't care what happened to me at all, not ever again. However, if it wasn't Carter, I might find myself in a very different, not to say dangerous, situation.

As I pondered, the cowled figure held the candelabra over the casket and, leaning forward, appeared to kiss the mannequin inside. Suddenly I knew that I could wait no longer. Taking a deep breath, I quietly pushed open the door. Carefully I got to my feet and, with my heart thudding hard enough to be heard across the room, moved cautiously toward the dark form in front of the coffin.

When I was about four feet away, I opened my mouth wide and screamed. The scream was meant to do two things: to wake Carter (I hoped) and Alexander and bring them charging into the room; and to make the cowled figure whirl around so that I could shine the light on its face.

The last part of my plan worked all right. It worked with frightening speed. The figure spun quickly, the great black cape swirling around it like the folding wings of a bat, and my shaking finger pushed the switch button on the flashlight.

Instantly, the head and the face were spotlighted.

Shock and disappointment battled in my mind. It was the face of Frankenstein that stared back at me from the dark frame of the hood. I could clearly see the patchwork flesh, the stitched lips. What I couldn't see was who was beneath that mask. I had been so positive that I would see the true face of our enemy when I turned on that light. Instead I was confronted by another mask, another maddening disguise.

We both stood frozen for a long dreamlike moment—I with my flashlight aimed at the creature's face, like a handgun; he with his arms in the air, holding aloft the candelabra. By now I was sure it was a man.

Then the words burst out of me, torn out by my inner anguish.

"Who are you?"

He laughed, a high-pitched mad sound, and flung the candelabra at me.

I reacted more swiftly than I would have thought possible. I jumped backward, but in so doing I lost my balance and dropped the flashlight. It struck my foot and I cried out. The next instant the figure was on me. I felt cruel fingers digging into my shoulder. Then a fist smashed into the side of my face, stunning me.

The next few minutes were a montage of jumbled sounds and only partially remembered events. I felt myself being lifted and carried. Since I felt something hard pushing into my diaphragm, I must have been carried over his shoulder. From somewhere distant I could hear voices calling my name, as my captor ran with me. Each jarring step drove the breath from my body. Perhaps I merely dreamed the voices calling my name?

Soon I lost consciousness.

When I finally became fully aware of my surroundings again, I also became aware of pain. My face ached abominably where I'd been hit. I was conscious of a dry musty smell. I finally opened my eyes and tried to figure out where I was.

I was in a room I had certainly never seen before; a small, circular room, with a low ceiling and no windows that I could see. The only light came from a candle in a ruby glass bowl suspended from the ceiling. The walls were paneled in dark wood and there was a blood-red carpet on the floor. The couch on which I lay was the only piece of furniture in the room.

My mind began to replay what had happened from the time I awoke from my doze in the closet in Nedra's room. Fear rose in me until I could almost taste the coppery flavor of it in my mouth. I elevated myself to a sitting position and, hardly aware of the painful throbbing in my face and head, looked quickly around the room.

Against the wall opposite me rose a shadow darker and bulkier than the others in the room. As I watched in horrified fascination, it moved and the livid scarred face of the Frankenstein monster looked at me. The stitched lips were caught in a permanent caricature of a smile.

The scream I felt rising in my throat would not come out. I could only watch numbly as it lurched toward me. It stopped in the center of the room and the large pale head wagged slowly from side to side. Then the creature raised a square-fingered white hand and waved a forefinger as if in admonition.

"You've been a bad girl, Molly," the creature announced in that high, sexless voice; the voice I was beginning to know so well. "Yes, you've been a bad girl, and bad girls must be punished."

The finger stopped wagging. I could feel that the person behind the mask was studying me intently, as if for some reaction, although in the dim light in the room I couldn't see past the mask into the eyes.

My vocal chords seemed frozen, but I knew that I had to speak. I had to try to gain some time, so that Carter and Alexander, so that *somebody*, could find me. Also, I realized that I was in the presence of madness. Perhaps that would work in my favor, gain me valuable time. If only I could get him to talk, keep him talking....

I tried to get my thoughts in order. "Why?" I finally managed. "Why have I been a bad girl?"

"Meddlesome! Meddlesome!" whined the voice. Then the monster abruptly sank to the floor and squatted there in front of me like a trick-or-treat nightmare, smiling and nodding that monstrous head.

"You have meddled into things that are none of your business, you see."

"What things?" I said faintly. "What things are you talking about?"

"Well, you married *him*," said the voice in a reasonable tone. "Didn't you? *Didn't you!*"

This last was said with a sibilant frightening intensity that sent chills up my arms and legs.

"Ye-s," I stammered. "But we love each other, Carter and I. Is that so wrong?"

"Yes!" the voice hissed. "Wrong! *Wrong!* You should have known better than to fall in love with a married man. A man who belongs to another!"

The Frankenstein head was nodding wildly now. I realized the creature was becoming highly agitated but I had to go on, not only to stall for time, but because now I knew that I was on the verge of finding out the secret of Trollhaugen, of finding out what this thing was that had touched our lives with venomous hands.

At the same time I had to fight back an impulse to giggle. The conversation was like a snatch of nonsense dialogue right out of "Alice in Wonderland". And yet... I knew there was some sort of weird logic to this creature's babblings, if I could only make sense of it.

"Carter was *not* a married man," I said as calmly as I could. "His first wife is dead. If you know anything at all about Carter, you should know that."

The creature jumped up and lumbered toward me. Then, just as the thought slid into my mind that I might possibly grab the mask and snatch it off, he stepped back, almost as if he knew what I was thinking.

"No!" he said loudly. "NO! NO, NO! Nedra is not dead. She is here, in this house, in her bedroom, resting as she always does after a difficult performance. Her death is a malicious rumor. A rumor spread by vicious people who hate her!"

I had to grab my arms to stop the sudden trembling of my body. There was such force, such passion in that voice! I felt as if I was being battered by the words, as if they were weapons. The voice itself, the tone and the nuances beneath the overlay of artifice, it sounded so familiar, *so* familiar...

"But Nedra didn't love Carter Faraday, you see," the voice said insinuatingly. The head was wagging again, but roguishly now, as if passing on a sly secret. The hairless white hands were folded together upon the left breast and the words slithered like snakes out of the twisting mouth.

"She had everybody fooled, you see. Nedra loved me. We were lovers. I know there were others but they were just toys, passing distractions to her. *I* was the one she really loved. *I* was the only man she ever truly, truly loved."

The large pale head nodded now, up and down, up and down. "Until *he* came along and took her away from me...if only *he* hadn't come along..."

He dropped to the floor again, like a horrible malformed child about to divulge secrets. "So I had to do what I had to do, you see. You do see, don't you?"

I nodded quickly, beginning to be afraid now, afraid of what I was going to hear.

"I understand," I said softly. "I really do. What...What was it that you did...?"

Frankenstein looked at me for a long moment, sitting perfectly still, and I literally held my breath until the voice came at me again.

"Why, I punished her, I punished Nedra," the voice said, sadly. "I had to, you see. I had to teach her a lesson. It was *me* she loved, not *him*. She was hurting both of us. So I punished her."

"How?" My voice faltered, and broke on the word.

The Frankenstein horror studied me again, as if trying to decide whether or not to confide in me further. Then the voice said very coldly, "I fixed the harness they used to hang her in that scene. I fixed it so that it would squeeze her slender white neck and cause her pain, as she was causing me pain. It didn't take long. The grips cut her down and placed her on the floor. Then they took her away. They tried to tell me she was dead but I knew they were lying, you see. They were trying to fool me. Nedra was trying to fool me. They all tried to fool me but, in the end, I fooled them, you see. I've fooled everyone..."

The monster rose slowly and, just as slowly, started toward me, those hands extended. At that moment, I knew I was close, very close to death. I screamed, I screamed as loudly as I could.

Then the pounding began and I heard the sound of shouting voices, distorted by the thick walls.

The figure advancing on me halted and whirled toward the sounds, then turned back to face me again.

"I will be back, Molly. I will be back to punish you."

He took a large iron key from beneath the folds of the robe. In a moment he had opened a door that I hadn't seen before and vanished behind it, locking the door on the other side.

The pounding had stopped now. I felt weariness and hopelessness settling around me like a shroud. Would they find me before this madman "punished" me the way he had Nedra?

I opened my mouth wide and screamed once again, screamed with all my might, but the sound was thin and futile hurled against the stone walls of the room. Then I glanced up at the low ceiling and it dawned on me where I was.

The tower! I was in a room under the tower! Of course, where else would there be a round room in Trollhaugen?

In the dim flickering light, I could see the faint outline of a trapdoor in the ceiling. I pushed and tugged the couch over beneath the outlined door and stood up on it. I held my breath and stretched my arms high, then breathed a sigh of relief. I could reach the ceiling easily enough. Logic told me that the trapdoor would be bolted but I hoped and prayed that it was not. Carefully, gently at first and then with all my might, I pushed against the trapdoor.

Chapter Sixteen

I kept pushing against the trapdoor as hard as I could. Soon my shoulders began to ache with the strain. My heart sank; it seemed to be bolted fast. Then suddenly, as I exerted the last bit of my strength, it popped open, almost causing me to lose my balance.

There seemed to be only darkness in the room above. For a moment I wondered if I would be placing myself in even more danger up there. Then, remembering what I would be facing if I remained in *this* room, I decided whatever was on the other side of the door couldn't possibly be any worse.

Since the ceiling was so low, I didn't have too much difficulty pulling myself up and through the trapdoor. Hoisting myself up until my bottom was resting on the edge of the opening, I tried to look around me. The darkness was total. Was I in another windowless room? Had I been wrong and this *wasn't* the tower room?

I pushed myself farther away from the edge of the trapdoor and felt all around me. In that moment I almost panicked, for my hands touched nothing but wood. Wood all around me, on all sides and above me. I had an appalling thought—Nedra's coffin! That thought pushed my already frayed nerves over the edge.

I began striking out blindly, wildly, in all directions and, in my struggles, I evidently struck some sort of latch or release. All at once the wooden lid above me swung up and back. Pale moonlight splashed over me and into the large chest in which I found that I was sitting.

I scrambled to my knees, then to my feet and looked around. I was in the tower room, right enough; the room where Carter and I had seen the shadow of the hanging figure. I was standing inside the huge carved chest that I had noticed that night in the middle of the floor. Now at least one mystery was cleared up. No wonder I hadn't found any trace of another doorway when I had searched the room that night. No wonder whoever had been in here had been able to vanish so quickly.

I didn't dare turn on the room light. However, the moonlight was sufficient for me to see well enough to close the trapdoor, clamber out of the chest, close that too and make my way toward the stairwell.

The stairwell was cold and I shivered in my thin blouse. The moonlight coming in through the tower windows up above gave me enough light. I slowly made my way down the stone steps, grateful for the fact that they didn't squeak and give me away.

At the base of the tower, I quietly pushed open the door and peeked out before I ventured into the hallway. Trollhaugen was ominously quiet, quiet as a grave. I shivered at the image.

But where on earth were Carter and Alexander? Did I dare call out to them?

I stood mouse-still for a minute or so, in a quandary. Should I try to make it to the bedroom upstairs? Of course it didn't seem likely that Carter was up there now. Hadn't I heard shouts and pounding? He and Alexander were almost certainly looking for me. Maybe I should flee, make a run for the garage, and try to get down the hill to the nearest neighbor. But the memory of the car accident made me hesitate. What if the brakes had been tampered with again? I also considered calling the police, yet I recalled how much Carter, and Alf, had been against that.

Then the decision was taken out of my hands. I heard something, or someone, coming toward me down the hall. It might be Carter, or Alexander. Or it might be *him*.

I didn't wait around to find out.

Very quietly, I tiptoed down the hall and slipped through the door into the Chapel. I slid the bolt home on the door behind me and, for the moment, breathed a little easier.

The Chapel was chilly and spooky looking, puddled with pools of colored light where the moonlight came through the stained-glass windows.

I heard footsteps down the hall. Holding my breath, I leaned against the cold stone wall and watched fearfully as the door knob turned quietly back and forth. I had no thought of calling out. But if the person on the other side of the door was Carter, or anyone else who belonged there, wouldn't *he* call out to me?

The side door, the one leading outside!

I had to make certain it was locked. Recklessly, I switched on one of the overhead lights. The sudden glare, after the near-darkness blinded me for a moment, and I stumbled against one of the seats, bumping my shin. I cried out. In a flurry of pain and panic, I ran the rest of the way to the outside door and found it already bolted.

After a little my pumping heart slowed a bit. I gasped for air, only now realizing how terribly tired I was. I must find some place to hide, to rest, but where? Whoever was after me surely knew this house better than I did.

Disconsolately, I made my way backstage, hoping to stumble onto some miracle—a weapon, a hiding place, anything.

At the back of the dressing room, I noticed a small cabinet that I didn't recall seeing before. I vaguely wondered if it was large enough to hide me. Then I saw something sticking out of the bottom of the door, a piece of fabric that looked familiar.

I pulled open the door and looked inside. It was full of costumes. One of which was Nedra's costume, the one Emma had pulled out of the trunk that day when she and Monica had come to borrow costumes for their party. The rest of the costumes seemed to be the same size. Were they all Nedra's?

Almost too tired to really care, I was about to close the door when I abruptly realized something odd.

The space where the dresses were hanging

didn't quite match the measurements of the outside of the cabinet. It must have a false back, I thought. I pushed the clothes aside and tapped gently on the back of the cabinet, producing a sound as hollow as a drum. I pulled the dresses helter-skelter from the rack and threw them behind me, almost wishing that Nedra was in one of them and that I could toss her memory aside so easily. When the cabinet was empty I looked for and found a button, just below the clothes bar. I pushed it, and the back of the cabinet slid noiselessly open.

Again I was facing a dark entrance but, eventually, my fumbling fingers found a light switch on the other side of the door. When the light came on, it illuminated another small windowless room. This one was square and there were all sorts of equipment and boxes piled against the walls.

For a moment I almost forgot my fear and my fatigue. It was clear to me that some of the items I saw could have been used to rig most of the phenomena Carter and I had seen. There was another dummy of Nedra, wearing a leather collar with a long rope attached. There were several lights of the spotlight variety used for out-of-doors. I saw rolls of wire and electrical parts. I saw a very large open make-up kit, as well as a row of costumes and masks hanging along one wall. These included the Witch, the Wolfman and Dracula. Only Frankenstein seemed to be missing and I had a good idea where that one was.

There was also a strange apparatus that I did not recognize at once. After some study, I decided that it must be a hologram projector. I had seen one once at a fair exhibit. That would explain the shadows of Nedra on the walls and the stage.

As I continued to look around the room I found that, while it was without windows, it did have another door. There was one set in the far wall. I caught myself looking toward it fearfully, wanting to know where it might lead yet afraid to find out. I moved slowly toward it.

I was in front of it, holding the cold brass knob in my hand, when I sensed someone behind me. Tensing, I turned slowly. There he was behind me, the huge patchwork head nodding and the horrible mouth with that sly permanent smile.

"Caught you, Molly," said the sexless voice. He shook a square white finger at me. "Oh, you will have to be punished now. I told you to stay in the room, you see, like a good girl. Oh, it was very clever of you to escape me like that."

As he spoke the last, he began to lumber toward me. I turned the door knob and yanked the door open, but he pounced on me before I could get the door wide enough to slip through.

"So we want to see where the door leads, do we? Well, it just so happens we are going in that direction, you see."

Grabbing my right wrist and my left shoulder, he twisted my right arm behind me and hard up against my shoulder blades. In this uncomfortable position, he propelled me ahead of him down the dark corridor. I could feel his breath hot against my ear and I could not escape the cold furry voice that told me in detail how I was going to die. I tried not to listen.

We were proceeding along a narrow dark corridor. I could see nothing in front of me and my shoulders kept bumping the walls on both sides. The corridor had a dank closed-in smell.

Finally the drone of his voice stopped for a moment and I gasped out, "Where are we going? Where are you taking me?"

"You'll find out soon enough," he said, and laughed, the sound echoing eerily.

"Carter will find you," I said. "I heard him calling when we were under the tower room."

My captor twisted my arm cruelly. I gasped and sagged from the pain, but he quickly hauled me to my feet and forced me on down the seemingly endless corridor.

After a few more stumbling steps, my foot struck something and I fell to my knees, bruising my shins against a sharp hard surface.

"Stairs," hissed the voice in my ear. "Climb, Molly. It won't be long now."

He jerked me to my feet. My shoulder and elbow blazed with the pain. In desperation, I opened my mouth and screamed as loudly as I could. The sound seemed to rebound down the narrow corridor like a banshee's wail.

My captor snarled an obscenity and I felt a blow against the side of my face. It partially stunned me. Having little fight left in me, I allowed myself to be pushed on up the steps without further protest.

It seemed as if I had been walking and

climbing forever. Still half-dazed by the cuff alongside the face, I finally realized we had stopped. The man behind me reached around me and I felt fresh air on my face. I breathed deeply, gratefully. A hard shove from behind sent me reeling forward, but at least he had let go of me. Numbly I wondered why, then I knew the reason. There was no place to run to, unless I could get past him and back the way we had come.

We were on the roof of Trollhaugen. I didn't want to think about the reason why he had brought me up here. Turning toward him, I backed slowly away. For the moment he did not even seem aware of my presence. Head cocked, he seemed to be listening to a voice or a sound that only he could hear. The moon flooded the rooftop with bright light.

And then that patchwork face swung in my direction once more, the stitched mouth caught in that perpetual smile.

"Well, here we are. Little Molly, pretty Molly. It's a shame that you didn't attend to your own affairs. It's a shame that you married Carter, you see, and got involved in all this. If you had never come to Trollhaugen..."

I rubbed my aching elbow and made an attempt to arrange my wandering thoughts. I was *so* tired, and so emotionally drained, that my mind kept drifting off on a tangent. I didn't seem to have the will to do anything but stand there and listen to that hateful voice coming at me.

"Well, Molly, have you nothing to say? Nothing at all?"

"Why?" I whispered. "Why must you do these crazy things? They'll catch you, you know. You'll spend the rest of your life behind bars."

The words poured out of me, but I was too tired to speak them with any passion. I almost didn't care what happened to me.

Then his hand lashed out and struck me across the face. "Crazy, am I?"

The blow stung just enough to jar me out of my apathy. Now I was filled with anger and hatred. I hated this grotesque figure with everything in me.

He was going on, shaking that horrible head from side to side. "Oh, no! They won't catch me. I am going to join Nedra, you see. *He* will be properly punished when you die. He will know what it's like to lose the one you love best in the world. He didn't really love her, you see. Not near the end. He had found out too much about her, about all the others."

"The others?"

"The other men, of course," the sexless voice said impatiently. "You see, *I* understood about them. I knew that she had to have her playthings, her distractions, her friendships. But *he* never understood. He was selfish. He wanted her for himself alone, that's why he married her. But she still saw them. She still saw me. He threatened her. He told her that if she didn't give up the others, he would leave her. And that's what I've never understood; she said she would. Nedra told me she wouldn't see me anymore. That was when I knew she had to be punished. But something went wrong. I only meant to hurt her, not drive her away from me. But she isn't dead. She isn't!"

His eyes blazed behind the eyeholes in the mask and he leaned toward me.

I found myself stuttering words of reassurance. "Of course not. I know. Nedra is waiting for you downstairs."

He seemed to relax a little, nodding. "Yes. Downstairs. I had to punish *him*, too. If it wasn't for him, I wouldn't have had to punish her, you see?"

"Yes, I see. I see."

"Then *you* came along, and he was happy again. He forgot about poor Nedra. He forgot all his suffering. He married you. He defiled her memory. When you are gone, he will suffer again."

The last words were spoken simply and quietly. I saw that he was lurching toward me again. Fear seized me. He was going to kill me now! I moved away from him, backing crab-fashion toward one of the chimneys.

He laughed a scratchy, climbing sound. "Going to hide from me again, Molly? No place to hide up here, you see."

The rooftop was washed with light from the full moon. The wind sighed and sang through the television aerial and around the chimneys. In the moonlight the Frankenstein figure loomed more like a fantasy creature than ever, a figment of my vivid imagination. I found that I had stopped wondering who was hidden beneath the costume. It seemed, in that moment, that the monster was an entity in itself, complete and autonomous and real, very real.

My back struck something hard. I was against the chimney. There was no place left to go.

He was only a few steps from me, when I heard a faint sound behind him. The door to the roof was slowly opening. I could not keep my gaze from the slowly widening gap. It couldn't be the wind, it couldn't be! Hope kindled a sharp little flame in me. He must have seen its reflection mirrored in my eyes because he whirled clumsily to look behind him.

As the wind whined around us and the moonlight illuminated the rooftop like a giant stage, Carter stepped out onto the roof. At least I thought it was Carter. It was a man Carter's height and he was dressed in the costume Carter had worn in "Drops of Water"; a tight-fitting black suit with trousers molded to his legs, and a short jacket that showed off his powerful physique. On his head was the now-famous mask; almost featureless, of polished silver, and the close-fitting black head-piece that gave his forehead a high domed look.

Behind him now came the others. All in costume: Wolfman, Batman, Witch, Snake-woman, Mist-woman. In the moonlight all looked as believable as reality to my startled eyes and evidently just as real to Frankenstein, who stood frozen staring at them. For the moment he was oblivious of me.

"It's all right now, Molly," said the tall figure. It was indeed Carter's voice, and I was never so glad to hear a familiar voice in my life. I felt the tension run out of me. My legs turned to water and I sank down onto the cold tar of the roof, with the chimney rough but very welcome against my back.

"It's all over, old friend." Carter moved slowly toward the figure of Frankenstein, whose shoulders slumped down now. I dimly noticed the Wolfman edging around behind his back, toward me.

"What are you all doing here?" the sexless voice said plaintively. "Go away! I must punish her. I must punish Molly. Then I can rest, you see, because then you will suffer too."

"All the punishment, all the suffering, is over, old friend," Carter said in a voice gentle with compassion. He extended a hand. "Come with us. We will help you."

"No!" The Frankenstein figure flinched away. "How did you all get here? How did you *know*?"

"We've known for some time, I think." It was a woman's voice from the group behind Carter. "Each of us, separately, has known or suspected. It is to our shame that we didn't tell Carter a long time ago, but none of us wanted to betray you."

"Yes," said another voice. Again, I wasn't sure who the voice belonged to. "Telling ourselves that it was in the name of friendship, we let terrible things happen. But at least we came to our senses in time to save Molly."

That seemed to galvanize the person in the Frankenstein disguise. He drew himself up. "You can't! You can't stop me!"

He had turned, while speaking, and was moving toward me. At that moment, the Wolfman ducked around from behind the chimney, scooped me up into his arms and leaped nimbly aside. As he did so, Carter and the others closed swiftly on Frankenstein.

With fatigue-dulled senses I watched what happened next. Frankenstein, with what seemed to me to be superhuman agility, sprang away from them and up onto the parapet of the roof. There, outlined against the moonlight, he pulled off that huge monster head. For the first time I saw the face of the person who had been intent on killing me.

It was Raul del Rio, but a Raul I had never seen. Face white and contorted with passion, eyes ablaze with madness, he glared at them and over at me. Then an abrupt change came over him, as if a giant hand had suddenly erased all the torment from his features and the madness from his eyes. His facial muscles relaxed and the face we saw was the face we all knew so well, handsome and mocking.

"I will go to Nedra now," he said quietly, so quietly I could barely hear him.

In an instant he was gone. The parapet was empty and the only sound, for an endless time, was that of the wind crying mournfully around the chimneys. Then a sickening thud sounded from below. I saw some of the people rush to the parapet to peer over.

I nearly fainted from the horror of that sound, but it was wiped away as I was passed from one pair of arms to another and I found a warm safe haven in the arms of my husband.

"How did you get them all here?" I whispered against Carter's chest.

He kissed my hair. "When I couldn't find you anywhere, I called them. I told them that, if any of them knew anything at all about this whole affair, now was the time to come with it."

"We're all sorry, Molly." It was Emma's voice. "I guess each of us had suspected all this was being done by Raul, but we had no proof. Strangely, we had never discussed it among ourselves. I guess we thought it would stop before any real harm was done...."

I raised my face from Carter's chest. "But you're all in costume, just like when the club is meeting."

In the moonlight I saw Emma's smile. "That was my idea. I thought maybe we could reason with Raul better. I'm afraid he's been living in some sort of fantasy world for some time now."

"It's all right," Carter broke in impatiently. "It's all over now. Why don't one of you call the police? Molly and I will be fine." He gazed down into my upturned face with loving eyes. "Won't we, darling?"

"We're going to be fantastic," I said in a voice choked with tears. I felt very thankful and happy because I knew it was the absolute truth, knew it deep in my heart.

I clung to Carter with all my strength. We stood locked together as the members of the Club Macabre began to move away with a murmur of hushed voices and the shuffle of footsteps.

I wondered if this was, perhaps, the last meeting of the Club Macabre. I hoped not. Now that the nightmare had passed, I would enjoy it more. But there were more important things to consider at the moment. Eyes closed, I raised my face, my lips seeking Carter's.

DISCARD